Nick considered Carolyn for a long second. She felt as if he could see past every wall she'd constructed, every bit of armor she'd put in place over the years.

He leaned down until his mouth met her ear. His breath whispered past a lock of her hair. "You look beautiful today, Carolyn."

Something hot raced through her veins. She refused to react to him, though her hormones didn't seem to be riding the same resolve wagon.

"Thank you."

He was still close, so close she could see the flecks of gold in his eyes. If she leaned a few inches to the right, she could touch him. Feel his cheek against h

From city girl—to corporate wife!

They're working side by side, nine to five....
But no matter how hard these couples
try to keep their relationships strictly professional,
romance is undeniably on the agenda!

But will a date in the office diary lead to an
appointment at the altar?

Find out in this exciting miniseries.

If you love office-romance stories, look out for

The Boss's Unconventional Assistant
by Jennie Adams
Coming in August

Crazy About Her Spanish Boss
by Rebecca Winters
in September

Hired: The Boss's Bride
by Ally Blake
in October

SHIRLEY JUMP

Boardroom Bride and Groom

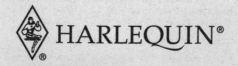

TORONTO • NEW YORK • LONDON
AMSTERDAM • PARIS • SYDNEY • HAMBURG
STOCKHOLM • ATHENS • TOKYO • MILAN • MADRID
PRAGUE • WARSAW • BUDAPEST • AUCKLAND

ISBN-13: 978-0-373-18384-5
ISBN-10:   0-373-18384-4

BOARDROOM BRIDE AND GROOM

First North American Publication 2008.

New York Times bestselling author **Shirley Jump** didn't have the willpower to diet, nor the talent to master under-eye concealer, so she bowed out of a career in television and opted instead for a career where she could be paid to eat at her desk: writing. At first, seeking revenge on her children for their grocery-store tantrums, she sold embarrassing essays about them to anthologies. However, it wasn't enough to feed her growing addiction to writing. So she turned to the world of romance novels, where messes are (usually) cleaned up before The End. In the worlds Shirley gets to create and control, the children listen to their parents, the husbands always remember holidays and the housework is magically done by elves. Though she's thrilled to see her books in stores around the world, Shirley mostly writes because it gives her an excuse to avoid cleaning the toilets, and helps feed her shoe habit. To learn more, visit her Web site at www.shirleyjump.com.

Praise for Shirley Jump

"Shirley Jump always succeeds in getting the plot, the characters, the settings and the emotions right."
—*CataRomance.com*

About *New York Times* bestselling anthology *Sugar and Spice:*
"Jump's office romance gives the collection a kick, with fiery writing."
—*PublishersWeekly.com*

On Shirley Jump's *The Other Wife:*
"Filled with humor and heart, this is a wonderful book."
—*Romantic Times BOOKreviews*

To my parents, who gave dozens of refugees a home in the United States and changed their lives forever. From them, I learned the value of opening your heart to those in need and that family is created, not always born.

CHAPTER ONE

CAROLYN Duff had made one major mistake in her life—a whopping cliché of a mistake in a Vegas wedding chapel—which hadn't, unlike the commercials said, stayed in Vegas.

It had followed her back here—and was working in an office just a few blocks down the street. All six-foot-two of him.

Most days she forgot about Nicholas Gilbert and concentrated on her job. As an assistant city prosecutor she barely had time to notice when the sun went down, because her days tended to pass in a blur of phone calls, legal precedents, Indiana case law and urgent e-mails. Her calendar might have said Friday, her clock already ticking past five, but still Carolyn stayed behind her desk, finishing up yet another flurry of work, even though tomorrow was the start of the Fourth of July weekend and the courts would be closed until Tuesday.

For Carolyn it didn't matter. An internal time

bomb kept ticking away, pushing her to keep going, to pursue one more criminal case, to see the prison bars slam shut once more.

To know she'd done her part again.

And yet it wasn't enough. Not nearly enough.

Carolyn rubbed at her temples, trying to beat back the start of another headache before it got too intense. Then she set to work, working on a negotiation for a plea bargain with a local defense attorney who thought his client—a petty thief—merited merely a ninety-day jail stint and a small fine. Carolyn, who could see the future handwriting on the wall, one that upped the ante to a felony charge—B&E with a deadly weapon—wanted years behind bars. The presiding judge, however, wanted a fast resolution that would clear his docket of one more hassle. He'd given the two attorneys the weekend to find a middle ground.

Mary Hudson popped her head in the door. Her chestnut pageboy swung around her chin, framing wide brown eyes and a friendly smile. "Everyone's gone home," said the paralegal. "Tell me you're taking the holiday weekend off, too."

"Eventually."

Mary sighed. "Carolyn, it's a holiday. Time to party, not work. Come on, go out for drinks with me. I'm meeting some of the girls from the other attorneys' offices over at T.J.'s Pub."

"Sorry, Mary. Too much work to do."

"You know what you need?" Mary crossed to the coffeepot on the credenza, adding some water from a waiting pitcher, then loading in a couple of scoops of coffee from a decorative canister, intuitively reading Carolyn's late-afternoon need for another caffeine fix. "A killer sundress and a sexy man—one always attracts the other."

When it came to fixing Carolyn up, Mary was like a persistent five-year-old wanting candy before dinner—she'd try every tactic known to man and wasn't above shameless begging. To Mary a woman without a man was akin to a possum without a tail—a creature to be pitied and helped.

"I don't need a man, Mary." Though the last time Carolyn had gone on a date…

Okay, so she couldn't think of the last time she'd gone on a date.

Speaking of dates and men—the image of Nick sprang to mind, and a surge of something thick and hot Carolyn refused to call desire rose in her chest. What was it with that man? He'd been a blip in her life story, and yet he'd always lingered in the back of her mind like he was the one chapter in her life she wished she'd never written but couldn't forget reading. Well, she certainly didn't intend to check that book out of the library again. She already knew the ending.

One crazy weekend. One reckless decision. Four days later it was over.

Mary leaned against the mahogany credenza, arms akimbo, waiting for acquiescence. "Okay, so I can't get you to leave early, but you will be at the fund-raiser for the Care-and-Connect-with-Children program, won't you? These kids are all so needy, Carolyn. I've seen their files. Foster kids, kids living below the poverty level—they run the gamut. And don't worry about having to get too involved or hands-on. We have a lot of activities planned to keep the kids busy all day, partly to give the foster parents a break, too. It's pretty overwhelming, taking in strangers."

And overwhelming for the children, living with strangers, but Carolyn didn't say that. She kept her past to herself. When she'd left Boston three and a half years ago, she'd also left those memories behind. "I promise, I'll be at the picnic on Saturday. But I don't need a new dress. I can wear the one I wore to the office summer party last year. No one remembers what anyone wears at these things, and I can go stag because I am perfectly capable—"

"Of taking care of yourself," Mary finished on a sigh. "Yeah, I know. So are hermit crabs, but you don't see them smiling, now, do you?"

"They're crustaceans, Mary. I don't think they have smiles."

"Exactly." Mary nodded, as if that validated her point.

In the two years Mary had worked in the office, Carolyn had yet to figure out what stratosphere Mary's mind was working on. Luckily, Mary typed at an ungodly speed and filed with an almost zenlike ability. As for the rest...

Well, Carolyn was twenty-eight and didn't need anyone to tell her how to live her life. Or to tell her she needed a man to take care of her. Not when there were more important things on her desk, like a thief.

She opened the thick manila folder before her and began reviewing the facts in the case again. If she got distracted for one second, she could miss something. A guilty man, for instance. This time it was Liam Pendant, a career criminal with an unregistered firearm in the glove compartment of his truck. His lawyer wanted her to go easy on him, but Carolyn disagreed. What if Liam had taken his crime a step further? Entered the house instead of just stolen the lawnmower out of the open garage? What if he'd taken the gun along? Used it on the homeowner who had caught him running down the driveway?

Instead of a simple burglary charge, she could be looking at another senseless tragedy, the result of a bad temper mixed with a gun.

And Carolyn knew all too well where that could lead. How a family could be destroyed in the blink of an eye. No, she decided, reviewing Liam's extensive rap sheet again, then closing the folder.

There would be no deal.

Mary took a seat on the edge of Carolyn's desk, depositing a mug of coffee before her. Carolyn thanked her and went on working. Mary laid a palm on the papers, blocking Carolyn's view. "Hon, an earthworm has more of a life than you do."

"Mary, aren't you paid to—"

"Assist, not direct you?" she finished.

Carolyn laughed and stretched in her chair. "I guess I've said that often enough."

"And I've ignored you often enough. But after two years together, I consider us friends. And as your friend, I have to say you're working too hard." She rose, crossed the room and opened the closed blinds, revealing the brightly lit city outside. "In case you haven't noticed, it's summer. People are out there enjoying the sun. Not staying inside like vampires."

For a second, Carolyn paused to turn around and admire the view. The burst of fire the afternoon sun cast over the downtown square, the busy stream of traffic leaving the city as people returned to their families or headed out of Lawford for the tranquility of the lakes that dotted the Indiana landscape.

"It's a perfect day," Mary said. "And it's going to be a perfect weekend for the program for the kids. They're going to love all the gifts and the—"

"Oh the gifts! Damn!" Carolyn rubbed at her temples. "I haven't bought a single present yet. I promised to sponsor one of those children and I totally forgot to get to the store. I'm sorry, Mary. These last few cases have been eating up every spare moment."

"There's always going to be another case," Mary said gently. "Will you please get out and enjoy the sunshine, Carolyn? I swear, all this climate-controlled air is frying your brain."

Carolyn rose and crossed to the window. For a second, she felt the warmth of the day, felt the special magic that seemed to come with summer days wrap around her heart. Her mind spiraled back to her childhood, to those first days out of school, running to greet her father when he got home from work, the endless bike rides they'd take, the times he'd push her on the backyard swing—*just one more time, Dad, please, one more time*—the games of catch that went long into the twilight hours. Once in a while they'd stay up late, watching for shooting stars or playing catch-and-release with fireflies.

Her throat caught, a lump so thick in the space below her chin, she couldn't swallow. *Oh, Dad.*

How she missed him, the ache hitting deep and sharp, from time to time.

Every summer with her father had been…incredible. It had been just the two of them, after her mother had been killed in a car accident shortly after Carolyn was born. Because of that, Carolyn and her father had shared a bond. A bond she missed, missed so very much there were days when she swore she could touch the pain.

After her father died when she was nine, she'd lost that feeling of joy, that anticipation of warm days, of long, lazy evenings. She'd started staying indoors, avoiding summer because everything had lost its magic. Trying to forget the very season she had enjoyed so much.

Then Nick had come along a few years ago and reminded her of the fun she used to have. Reminded her that magic still existed.

For a while Carolyn had let loose and done something completely crazy—so crazy that it had led her to a disaster of a marriage. For five minutes she'd let go of the tight hold she'd had over her life, and when she had, the ball of control went rolling over the hill way too fast.

Thankfully, she'd fixed that mistake almost immediately, and everything was on the right path now. She was successful at her job. Sure, it had come at the cost of what other people had—a home, kids, the trappings of tradition—but for a woman like Carolyn, who had about as much experience with the traditional life as a swimsuit model did with dog sledding, it was just as well. Besides, neither she nor Nick had taken the marriage seriously, not really.

And when that face from her past appeared on the TV screen in the diner, blasting Carolyn's history on national airwaves, she'd made her choice and walked away from Nick for good.

Carolyn pushed away the memories then returned to her desk, swallowed two aspirin with the black coffee, and went back to work. "I'll leave early—er. I promise, Mary."

Mary sighed. "Okay. See you tomorrow, then. You will be at the picnic, right? Not chained to this desk?"

Carolyn smiled. "I'll be there. I promise."

"I'm holding you to it. And if you don't show up," Mary said, with a warning wag of her index finger, "you know I'll come right down here and drag you out of this office."

Mary said goodbye, then headed out of the office, already exchanging her pumps for a pair of flip-flops in her purse. Clearly, the paralegal was ready to start her holiday weekend.

Carolyn thought of the last time she'd done something that carefree. That spontaneous. And she couldn't remember. Somewhere along the road, it had simply become easier to spend weekends, holidays, Friday nights at her desk. Easier to ignore the invitations to dinners that were clearly fix-ups, the dates with men who didn't interest her, the lonely evenings at home by herself.

Mary was right. Carolyn could almost feel her father looking down on her from heaven, tsk-tsking at all the sunshine she had missed, the sunsets that had passed behind Carolyn's back as she'd worked.

Well, she *did* have shopping to do for the picnic tomorrow. What better excuse to leave early? She finished up the last few tasks on her desk, including leaving a voice mail for Liam's attorney telling him no deal, then shut down her computer. Her gaze caught on the bright blue-and-yellow envelope for the Care-and-Connect-with-Children program. She tugged it out, stuck it in her brief-case, then headed out the door.

As she headed down in the elevator, she opened the envelope and pulled out the photo of the child inside. A paper clip held a four-by-six-inch picture of a five-year-old boy to the corner of a sheet of paper.

Her stomach clenched. Oh, he was a cute little thing—blond and blue-eyed, a little on the skinny side, and in desperate need, the sheet said, of almost everything. School supplies, clothes, sheets. His dream wish list was so simple, it nearly broke Carolyn's heart: books to read and a single toy truck.

For a split second, she saw the future that could have been in the boy's eyes. If she had stayed married to Nick—if either of them had made that bond into something real.

Carolyn traced the outline of the child's face. What if…

But no. There were no what ifs, not where she and Nicholas Gilbert were concerned. Carolyn had made her choices, and made them for very good reasons—and exactly the one that made her happy.

By the time the elevator doors whooshed open, Carolyn was back in work mode. She'd deal with this sponsorship project with her typical take-charge attitude. Clutching the envelope tight, she ran down a mental list of tasks, compartmentalizing the entire process, treating it as simply one more thing to do. Distancing herself, keeping emotions out of the equation.

That, Carolyn knew, was the best way to protect her most valuable asset—the one she'd vowed never to expose again, especially not to another lawyer—

Her heart.

The last place Nick Gilbert expected to be on a Friday night was a toy store.

Yet here he was, standing in the center of a brightly lit aisle filled with pink and lace, trying to decide between a doll that cried and a doll that burped. To him, neither seemed to offer an advantage. Burping might be a cool and very funny option—but only if you were a teenage boy looking to crack up the algebra class. Nevertheless, given the way the little girls swarming around him were grabbing the toys off the shelves, both outbursts were wildly popular.

Cry…or burp?

He may have grown up in a big family, but everything Nick knew about children could fit on the back of an ant, with room left for an entire kindergarten class. Why had he agreed to sponsor a child for the Care-and-Connect-with-Children program? What was he thinking?

He'd been swayed by a picture. By the list of needs on the sheet inside the packet of information about the child. And he'd thought, with his typical can-do attitude, that he could handle this.

Ha. He'd have been better off trying to corral a herd of elephants.

And, truth be told, he'd also thought a trip to a toy store, a few gifts thrown into a cart and an afternoon at the Care-and-Connect picnic might fill the gnawing hole in his chest. It had grown more persistent lately, like a thirst he couldn't quite quench. A crazy feeling, because he should be content. He had everything he needed. A good career. Great friends, a loving family who lived nearby. An easy lifestyle that demanded nothing.

And yet…

His grip tightened on the dolls' try-me buttons, which made them let out a simultaneous burp-cry. Two moms in the aisle turned to look at him, twin amused smiles on their face, coupled with looks of compassion. A man in the baby doll aisle. Apparently he was an object of pity.

"Trial run before I have a real kid," he joked. "I think I like the burping better. It's more entertaining."

The moms shook their heads, then laughed and walked away.

Nick tossed both packages into his cart, then swung it around and headed down the aisle. He spun to the right, intending to get out of the store as quickly as he could. This was *so* not his forte. But as he rounded the corner, his cart collided with another, jostling the dolls, who complained with another burp-cry.

Nick barely noticed. Because he found himself staring at the one woman he thought he'd managed to forget.

Carolyn Duff.

She had deep-green eyes, so wide and dark,

they were as inviting as placid lakes beneath a moonlit sky. A charcoal suit hugged her body, yet gave nothing away. Sensible pumps with kitten heels, not high enough to show off the real curves of her long legs, but enough to remind him of those gorgeous, long limbs. Blond hair, put back in a severe, tight bun, but Nick knew, when she let her hair down, it would be just long enough to tease around her features and whisper along her cheekbones, her jaw.

Everything about Carolyn on the outside was delicate, and yet on the inside she was strong—like a flamingo that could weather a hurricane.

She'd been the one woman who had intrigued him more than any other in law school. Her upper-crust, stiff Bostonian attitude had been a challenge to him—because when they'd met and he'd made her laugh, he'd glimpsed the Carolyn underneath, it had made him want to peel back the layers, get her to loosen up. Tease out the fun side of the severe, break-no-rules studier.

He'd done that, then done the most spontaneous thing in his life. Taken it to the next level and married her—the biggest mistake of his life.

And now that mistake was standing right in front of him.

CHAPTER TWO

"WHAT are you doing here?" Carolyn asked. Her heartbeat doubled with the shock of seeing him. She saw the same surprise reflected in the widening of his eyes, the way he seemed rooted to the spot. Nick Gilbert, the last man she expected to run into in the toy aisle.

Nick. Her...

Husband?

The thought ran through her in a rush, along with the embarrassing memory of when she'd said "I do" in a tacky Vegas wedding chapel and made promises she, of all people, shouldn't have made.

No, he wasn't her husband. Not anymore. Her ex.

Their marriage, their relationship was over now. *They* were over.

"I was about to ask you the same thing," he said.

She looked up at him, hating the disadvantage of being shorter. At six-two, Nick had always had a good seven-inch height advantage over her.

Years ago she'd liked that. Liked that she could look up into his teasing blue eyes and be swept up into the humor of his smile.

But not anymore. Right now she wished she had on platform heels so she could go toe-to-toe with those blue eyes.

Blue eyes that no longer had any effect on her. Whatsoever. Despite the tingle she'd felt when she ran into him in the crowded courthouse elevator last week. And glimpsed him in the cafeteria from time to time.

She'd seen him off and on many times since their divorce, but never this close. Never had to have a real conversation with him. Even now, as she had for the past three years, she could turn away, walk down the aisle as if nothing had happened.

But something had. A little something inside her had zigged when they had zagged.

With a start, she realized he was staring at her—because she hadn't answered the question. Heat filled her cheeks, which only left her more discomfited.

Carolyn Duff didn't do discomfited. She *never* felt out of sorts.

"I'm buying toys for one of the children in the charity—" She glanced down at his cart and saw toys. Books.

"Me, too. I think the entire Lawford legal community got onboard with this one," he said. "But maybe I should have stuck to business law. I haven't the foggiest idea what the hell I'm doing." He reached into his cart and pulled out the two dolls. "Burps or cries? Which is better? How am I supposed to know? To me, they're both losing propositions."

She laughed and when she did, it resurrected a part of her she'd thought she left behind long ago. A lightness she'd lost in the years she'd lived with her aunt Greta, then rediscovered when she'd met Nick.

A lightness she'd missed in the heavy work of being a city prosecutor.

She glanced at Nick. The poor man clearly had no clue when it came to kids—and neither did she. The two of them were stuck in the same shopping hell. What harm could come from a little talking? "I know exactly how you feel. I was standing in the next aisle with the same problem." She reached into her cart and pulled out a selection of trucks. "Fire engine or police car? Dump truck or…what is this thing? A front loader? And what is a front loader anyway? And then there's these things called transformers, but I can't figure out why anyone would want a toy that transforms, or if it's even what this boy would want." Carolyn tossed the toys back into her cart and threw up her hands. She was babbling. She always did that when she got nervous—something that only seemed to happen outside the courtroom, and apparently whenever she got around Nick, who was a six-foot-two reminder of her biggest mistake. "Whatever happened to a bat, a ball and a catcher's mitt?"

Nick chuckled. "It has gotten complicated, hasn't it? Every single thing I see here has a computer chip in it, I swear. These aren't just toys, they're technological revolutions." Nick shook his head. "Well, I'll muddle through somehow. After all, I've got a college degree. How hard can it be? Just watch me." He chuckled, showing the easy humor that had always been as much a part of Nick as his dark-brown hair and his cobalt eyes.

Did he remember that crazy decision to rush off to Vegas? The heady choice they'd made? One where they'd clearly not been thinking with brain cells, and only with the blush of lust?

Carolyn, out of Aunt Greta's house for the first time since she was nine, so desperate to cast off the strangling structure of her past, saw escape in Nick. She'd married him for all the wrong reasons and had at least been smart enough to undo it the first chance she got.

Nick leaned forward, reading the boxes that lined the shelves, studying the facts and figures, researching his purchase. He was being the detail man that made him a good lawyer, but betraying none of the funny, spontaneous Nick she'd once known. Just as well. She didn't need that man in her life. Because that man was the one who had— for a snippet of time—made her think she could be someone she really wasn't.

"This says ages eight and up," Nick read aloud, sounding as serious as a tax accountant. "I don't think that will work. My paper says the child is six."

"My—" She caught herself before she said "my child," because this wasn't her child. "The child I'm sponsoring is almost the same age. I have a five-year-old."

"Someone wasn't thinking. Giving you and me a couple of little kids like that. They should have assigned us two high school students. *That* we can handle. Buy them a couple calculators and some dictionaries. Sit them down, dispense some college advice."

"Yeah." She let out a little laugh. An uncomfortable silence filled the space between them, the kind that came from two people who used to know each other and now didn't, who were pretending everything was cool—even when a heat still simmered in the air.

Leave, her mind said. Take this pause as what

it was—an excuse to go. But her feet didn't go anywhere and she couldn't have said why.

"Maybe you should try this one." Carolyn picked up a box that held a big white plastic horse designed for a doll to take galloping into the sunset. She flipped over the box, read the same age recommendation as Nick had seen and put it back on the shelf. That was all they needed—a choking lawsuit. "Forget it. Too many small parts."

He gave her a smile. "When did you get so smart about toys?"

"I didn't. It's the lawyer in me reading the fine print."

"You always were good at that part."

Carolyn let those words go, knowing Nick meant more than the directions on a box. She'd been the strict one, always playing by the rules, where he'd been the opposite.

"What's your kid's name?" Nick asked, strolling further down the aisle, toward the dress-up clothes.

"Name?" Carolyn looked at him.

"Yeah. His or her name."

"Uh…" Carolyn thought for a second. "Bobby."

Nick grinned, and when he did, Carolyn was whisked back to those college days. "Nice name. My child is named Angela."

"Your…your child? You're married?"

"Are you kidding me? Could you see me with

kids?" He chuckled. "You know me, Carolyn. I'm not the kind of guy who likes to have ties."

That had been part of the attraction and part of the problem. Carolyn had gone for Nick because he'd been the complete opposite of the life she'd left in Boston, but when she'd needed him to be dependable, to listen, to be a true partner—

He hadn't been there. He'd let her down.

"No, I never married again," Nick went on. "Angela is the child I'm sponsoring."

Carolyn released a breath she hadn't even realized she'd been holding. Nick wasn't married. He didn't have kids. No other woman had laid claim to his heart.

She shouldn't care. The days when she had any stake in Nick—or in anything about Nick— were long past.

"So, nope, no kids for me. This is as close as I get." He gestured toward the basket of toys.

"A one-day commitment, huh?"

"Those seem to be the kind I'm good at." Nick's gaze met hers, and their shared history unfurled in the tension thickening the air between them.

A mother with two children, one strapped into the shopping cart's seat, the other trailing behind and whining discontent about some toy she'd been denied, squeezed past them. On the overhead sound system, someone called for a price check in aisle three. Once again, the uncomfortable silence of two people who had essentially become strangers grew between Carolyn and Nick, like a tangle of thorny vines separating once-friendly neighbors.

"Well, it was great seeing you, Nick," Carolyn said. "Good luck with your shopping."

Before she could turn away, Nick reached out and laid a hand on top of hers. Carolyn took in a breath, the air searing her lungs, awareness pumping through her veins. Nick's touch, so familiar, yet also so new after all this time apart, spread warmth through her hand. The scent of his cologne—the same cologne, as if nothing had changed, not a single thing. The sound of his heartbeat, his every breath—could she really hear that, or was it just her own, matching his?—time stopping for one, long slow second. "Wait. Don't go," he said.

"Why?"

"Why don't we shop together?"

The mother and two children disappeared around the corner, the whine of the eldest child dropping off when she apparently spied a better toy. The store's music droned on with its instrumental rendition of Seventies hits, a soft undertow of lounge melodies. "Shop together?" Carolyn repeated.

He grinned. "Do either of us look like we know what the heck we're doing?"

She glanced down at her haphazard selection of toys. A complete zoo of stuffed animals. Every type and kind of truck carried by the store. Books that featured cartoon characters, superheroes, animals and dancing vegetables. She'd pretty much bought one of everything, hoping that a scattershot of presents would result in something the child might like.

She'd already spent three hours at this toy shopping and had almost nothing that said "Wow, great gift" to show for her efforts. Every item she picked up, she hemmed and hawed over, wondering if a little boy would like this or would prefer that. The truth was, she had no idea what little boys, or little girls, for that matter, really wanted. She could barely remember her own childhood.

When it came to buying presents for a little boy, who better to ask for an opinion than a male? A male who'd been the kind to enjoy playing Frisbee and catch on the college campus? The kind who clearly knew how to have fun?

She and Nick were both adults. Their marriage—which they'd both agreed back in that diner was a mistake—was far in the past. This was a charity mission. What harm could a few minutes of shopping do?

"This is a one-time offer," he said. "One of

the Lawford attorneys offering to help a prosecutor, pro bono."

She laughed again, and right there, found herself caught in the old spell all over again. The one that had made her abandon her structured life and go along with Nick's crazy Vegas plan. But this idea wasn't crazy; it was merely a partnership. "How very charitable of you."

"It's not charity. After all, weren't we always better together than apart?"

"Maybe in school, in classes, we worked well together, but not as a couple. You know that, Nick," she said. "As far as I'm concerned, we've been happily divorced for three years."

He arched a brow, cynicism written all over his features, and she wondered if maybe the end of the marriage hadn't been the relief to him that she'd always told herself it had been. "Happily?"

"Divorce was what we both wanted. We agreed it was a stupid mistake and the best thing was to undo it as fast as possible. Tell no one, forget it ever happened. Pretend we'd never met. Remember?" Carolyn remembered those words, the argument that had accompanied that moment, and most of all, the look of pained disappointment in Nick's eyes. It had surprised her, because she'd thought Nick hadn't taken their bolt to the altar seriously at all— hadn't thought Nick took anything seriously.

"I remember our ending as being more like removing a bandage, quick and a little painful."

"Well, it's over now, and we've both moved on, right?"

"Of course. And presumably, we've matured since then."

"Have you?" she asked.

He grinned. "Not a bit."

She chuckled. "I'm not surprised."

"Ah, but that's what keeps my life fun. And makes for entertainment in the courtroom."

She just shook her head. Nick was exactly the same.

Over the years, Carolyn had managed to avoid seeing Nick, as much as was possible in the relatively small Lawford legal community. It helped that they worked in two entirely different areas of law—criminal and corporate.

When they did see each other, they exchanged nothing more than a simple nod, a few words of greeting.

Wearing a suit, he was devastatingly handsome. Powerful. In boxers and bare-chested, he was—

Irresistible. Sexy.

Luckily, today he was wearing a two-button navy suit with a white shirt and dark-crimson tie. It fit him perfectly, hugging over the broad shoulders and defined chest she knew existed beneath the fine fabrics. As did, apparently, the rest of the female population in the store, women who made little secret of staring at Nick. And why not? Nick Gilbert was the kind of man women noticed.

Carolyn returned to the matter at hand, drawing herself up. "I'll let you get back to your shopping," she said. "It was nice to see you again. Good night, Nick."

She made moves to leave, but Nick took a step closer. "You don't want to shop together? Are you afraid?"

"Afraid of what?"

"Working together. Don't tell me the great Bulldog of Lawford isn't up to the challenge of a little shopping trip with her ex. For a good cause, I might add."

Her chin went up a notch. "I can certainly shop with you."

"And not be at all affected by my winning personality." He grinned. And damn if that smile didn't whisper a temptation to take a dip in the pool of fun again. Just for a second.

"What winning personality?" She gave him a slight teasing smile back. "I heard you lost your last two cases."

"Are you keeping track of my career, Miss Duff?"

"Of course not."

"One might think you are. Otherwise, why

would a city prosecutor care what a corporate lawyer is up to?"

Her chin rose a little higher. "Just making sure you're staying in check, Mr. Gilbert, and not breaking any rules."

He grinned. "And when have you ever known *me* to stay in check?"

The memory danced into the forefront of her thoughts. The first time she'd met Nick Gilbert. She'd been leaving the university library, over-loaded and overwhelmed, books piled in her arms, preparation for a marathon study session for the upcoming bar exam.

She'd transferred to the Indiana school just a month earlier, and found the transition to be dif-ficult, the adjustment harder than she'd expected. She'd made the best of the change, as she always had of every situation in her life—because she didn't have a choice.

She'd been financially cut off in Boston and had opted for the only school that had offered her a partial scholarship and a tuition she could afford.

But she'd had difficulty fitting in among the informal Midwesterners who didn't understand the stiff-upper-lip Bostonian. One month in, and Carolyn had yet to make any friends. As she'd crossed the campus, she'd felt the stares of the other students. Her step had caught on a bump in the sidewalk, the books began to fall—

And then Nick Gilbert came along.

He'd stood out in a sea of brown and navy like a neon sign. He'd rushed over, righted the books and done the most insane thing she could have imagined to set her at ease.

He'd made a quarter disappear.

But in that simple, unexpected magic trick, Nick had won her over and made everything Carolyn had to face seem so much less daunting.

"So, what'll it be?" Nick asked. "Tough it out on our own in the wilds of the toy department or join forces?"

Carolyn met Nick's gaze and smiled, caught up in the old magic once again. "All right, I'll shop with you, but only because you are so clearly hopeless at this."

"Oh, I see, take pity on the man. Is that it?"

A bubble of laughter escaped her, filling Carolyn with a lightness she hadn't felt in weeks, months. How she craved that feeling, yet at the same time, felt the urge to flee. "Don't you *need* pity, Mr. Burp-or-Cry?"

"Oh, I need more than that, Carolyn."

The way he said her name, with that husky, all-male tone, the kind that spoke of dark nights, tangled sheets, hot memories, sent a thrill running through Carolyn, sparked images she'd thought she'd forgotten. But, oh no, she hadn't forgotten at all. She'd merely pushed those pictures to the side, her mind waiting—waiting for a moment like this to bring them to the forefront, like an engine that had idled all this time.

How she wished she were in a courtroom instead of a toy store. That was the world she knew, could predict. But Nick Gilbert was about as predictable as a tiger in a butcher shop.

This was a bad idea. A very bad idea.

"Playing house," Carolyn said, popping into action. "That's what we need."

Nick arched a brow. "You and me? Play house? I thought we already tried that and it didn't work so well."

"Not us. For…" Her mind went blank. Looking at Nick, thinking of playing house…oh, why had she thought she could do this? Just being here was a mistake. But she'd already made the deal and couldn't renegotiate. Not with a lawyer and especially not with this one. "I meant for the child you're sponsoring. Little girls, they like to play house. Pretend to go to the grocery store, set the table, all that."

"But not you, right, Carolyn? Or did you ever have a moment when you did play house? When you imagined being a Mrs. for longer than a few days?"

"Me?" She snorted. "You know that is so not me. I don't think I have a domestic bone in my body."

"We still have that in common," Nick said. "I've yet to become domesticated myself, though I am housebroken." He grinned. "What about you? How have things been for you over the last three years?"

Carolyn reached for the nearest toy on the shelf. "How about this broom set for Angela?"

"I recognize this avoidance tactic. Divert attention from the personal and get back to work, right?"

"Nick, if you're not going to take this seriously—"

"Oh, I'm serious, Carolyn." He straightened, his demeanor slightly chilled. "As serious as you are."

Then he started pushing the cart, heading down the aisle toward the faux food and make-believe vacuum cleaners. Now also all business and no play. Not anymore.

Carolyn wasn't the least bit disappointed. Not the least.

"How about this for Angela?" Nick held up a pretend cooking set, plastic frying pans, spatulas, bright yellow faux eggs and floppy bacon. Little cardboard boxes of cereal marched up the side of the package, with cheery pretend names like Cocoa Crunchies and Corn Flakies.

"Perfect," Carolyn said, coming up beside Nick and holding the other side of the package. Only a few inches separated them. When she inhaled, she caught the scent of his cologne again. She could sense the heat from his body, read the strength in his hands. She focused instead on the bright happy packaging, on the images of children sitting around a plastic table, pretending they were dining at a five-star mock-up restaurant. "When I was a little girl, they didn't make toys like this. I was always taking the real thing out of the kitchen and if I didn't have any friends over, I made my poor dad sit down for pretend meals. Oh, how I made that man suffer through tea parties with me and my bears."

Nick chuckled softly. "My sisters used to try to do the same thing to me and my brothers but we were too fast. We'd steal the cookies and run like hell for the yard. Linda, Marla and Elise still think Daniel and I are the spawn of the devil because we ruined their plans to recreate the Mad Hatter's Tea Party."

Carolyn laughed. "I never did get a chance to meet your family. I wish I had. They sound so fun."

"They would have liked you."

The words hung between them. They'd been married too short a time for meeting families—not that there'd been anyone on Carolyn's side to meet. Anyone who would have cared about meeting Nick, anyway.

Had Nick told his family about her? Had he told his sisters about the woman who had stolen his heart, then broken it, all in the space of a month?

Carolyn shoved the thoughts away. She'd had good reasons, reasons Nick had refused to see at the time, refused to listen. He'd fought her, tooth and nail, telling her it could wait, that they'd just gotten married—*stay awhile, don't go, not yet*— and not understanding at all that she'd *had* to go—

Had to get on that plane. She couldn't sit in Indiana, acting the part of the happy wife, while the man who had killed her father went on another rampage. By the time she came home, the divorce was final. Nick had done the filing, taking care of the details, cleaning up the mess.

It was all for the best, she told herself again

"Let's get the rest of Angela's gifts," Carolyn said, returning to business. Nick seemed relieved to do the same, and they made quick work of filling the cart with toys for the little girl.

"My turn to help you," Nick said a little while later. "And for your information, little boys don't want to play house, so let's pick a different aisle."

Work again. Concentrate on the project. Not the man.

Carolyn led the way as they headed over to the aisle of trucks and cars. Nick directed her toward the larger, more indestructible options. "This is what Bobby wants." Nick hoisted up a red plastic truck large enough to transport a puppy.

"How do you know for sure? There's this one, and that one, and the one down there." Carolyn gestured all over the aisle, as confused as she had been an hour ago.

"I know because I was once a little boy. And I had one of these, except mine sported the less-knee-and-elbow-friendly metal finish." Nick turned the box over in his hands, lost in a memory. "I had a lot of fun with that truck. I remember the Christmas I got it. I was five. Daniel was three. He came charging at me, wanting to play with the truck. Cut his chin open on the coffee table and he ended up in the emergency room on Christmas day, getting stitches."

"Oh, my goodness. That must have been awful."

Nick shook his head. "My mother is a saint. She could raise all five of us and run a household blindfolded. She shot off directions to my dad and the rest of us for how to put together Christmas dinner, loaded Daniel in the car and drove to the hospital, calm as a summer breeze. We, of course, butchered dinner without her there." Nick laughed. "But when she came back, with Daniel all stitched up, she somehow made it all right and saved Christmas."

Carolyn spun the loose plastic covering on the

shopping handle. She thought of how her aunt Greta would have reacted to such an event. For one, it wouldn't have happened because there'd been no big happy family around the Christmas tree. No turkey to stuff. No hectic gathering. But if there had been, Greta simply wouldn't have allowed chaos to disrupt her house. In Aunt Greta's house, chaos never, ever visited. It didn't even walk down the sidewalk. And secondly, children didn't take chances. They didn't run. They didn't ride their bikes down the sidewalk. They didn't do anything death defying. "Your family sounds like something out of a novel."

Nick smiled, then put the toy truck into the shopping cart. "Sometimes I think it was." Nick paused midstep, then met her gaze, and for a fleeting second she wondered if he was reading her mind. "Carolyn—"

"Let's get this shopping done. I need to get home. I have a ton of work waiting for me." Carolyn started down the aisle, cutting off Nick and the attraction she read in his gaze.

Then the look disappeared, gone in a simple blink.

"Yeah, good idea. We *should* concentrate on the shopping," Nick said, joining her by the race cars. "I have work waiting for me, too."

Carolyn gave him a sidelong glance but couldn't read anything in Nick's face. Maybe she had read Nick wrong. Or maybe he had changed, maybe he wasn't the man she remembered.

They finished the shopping trip, agreeing on their purchases easily. Before long, they'd found several hundred dollars worth of toys, much more than they'd expected to find or spend. The shopping spree had been fun, almost like—

Like when they'd gotten married. Never before had Carolyn gone without a plan, running by the seat of her pants, working purely on desire.

She hadn't been thinking that week, simply *doing*. And for a moment she'd thought she could do it all. Be a wife, and maybe…down the road… a mother.

What if today's toy buying hadn't been a charity mission? What if they'd been shopping for their own child?

Where would they be now? Living in a three-bedroom house in some subdivision in Lawford, kissing each other goodbye over a cup of coffee every morning? Or would they have ended up exactly where they were—divorced, scarcely cordial colleagues? Nick still acting a lot like a college frat boy, Carolyn still the stiff Bostonian?

"Those kids are going to need a truck to haul all this home," Nick said, interrupting her thoughts.

Carolyn smiled. "I think I saw some of those in aisle three."

"Don't tempt me," Nick said, and in his eyes, she read more than just the desire to buy a ride-on toy.

There was a lingering desire for her. Still burning in his gaze. Emanating from his skin, his nearness. And who was she kidding? She still felt it, too.

But the past was over. And for a good reason.

They'd made a big mistake once. Only an idiot did that twice.

"Well, I guess that's it. I, ah, can run over to the department store and pick up some clothes and sheets, if you want to take care of this stuff," Carolyn said, digging into her purse for money and then handing him half the cost of their purchases. Nick had agreed, since he had the bigger vehicle, to transport the toys to the picnic while she brought the other items. "See you tomorrow?" She tried to keep her tone as professional as it would be with a client.

As she turned to go, Nick took a step toward her, bringing them within inches of each other. Heat tingled down her spine, igniting a fire that had been dormant for a long, long time. For a second, she wondered if he were about to kiss her. Some crazy part of her wanted him to do just that. The same crazy side that had acted without thinking back in college.

Okay, probably not the best part of her brain to listen to.

"Carolyn," Nick said quietly.

"What?" The word escaped her in a breath.

"Don't go. Not yet. Grab a drink with me. Catch up on old times."

Oh, how easy it would be to let herself get caught up in him again. But no, she was older. Smarter now.

"Why, Nick? What's changed, really? You never really got serious about us. And I was always going to put my career first. Never the twain shall meet, isn't that what Shakespeare said?"

"There was more to our breakup than just that, Carolyn. Much more," he said, his eyes still on hers, his mouth inches away.

Despite her words, for a second she wanted very much for the twain to meet. For this pounding need to be quieted.

The rational half of her said this was desire, nothing more. At the same time, the feeling unnerved her, toppled her off her carefully planned and organized pedestal. She had no room in her days for a man like him—a man who would distract her, turn her from the very work that fulfilled her sense of self.

She hadn't the time then, she still didn't have it now. Sharing a drink with him wouldn't solve that dilemma.

"You're right," Carolyn said. "And all those reasons are still there, Nick."

The temperature in the aisle dropped a few degrees. "As always, you make a compelling case, Counselor. Well, tomorrow then." He turned to go, heading for the cash register.

As she watched him disappear, Carolyn told herself she was glad she'd turned down Nick's invitation. Because Nick Gilbert was a much-too-appetizing bowl of chocolate and cherry ice cream, and Carolyn was definitely feeling lactose intolerant.

CHAPTER THREE

NICK stood in the kitchen of his three-bedroom house and wrestled with the iron, cursing whoever had invented the damned thing. "Remind me again why I'm going to this shindig."

"Because you're a guy who cares about kids," said his brother, Daniel, who was making his regular visit to Nick's house. He'd already raided the fridge, complained about the dearth of acceptable meal choices, flipped through Nick's DVD collection twice and taken two of the newer flicks, as if Nick's house was Blockbuster. Nick didn't complain. He liked the company, and tolerated his brother's intrusions. Most of the time.

A writer, Daniel had the same dark brown hair and blue eyes as most of the Gilberts, but preferred a more relaxed approach to clothing, meaning anything fancier than jeans didn't exist in his closet. "And you better," Daniel added. "You grew up with four brothers and sisters."

"I didn't mean about the kids, I meant, why am I attending an event where Carolyn's going to be?" Earlier, he'd told his brother about running into Carolyn at the toy store.

A coincidence? Or a second chance with the woman he had never really forgotten?

Nick cursed the iron again as the steam sent globs of water over his shirt. "What is it with these things?"

"Didn't Mom teach you how to take care of yourself before she released you into the wild?" Daniel slid into place beside his brother. "Here, let me do it. For Pete's sake, you're making a mess of it."

Nick stepped back, amazed that his younger brother could wrangle the machine into doing his will. In five minutes Daniel had the golf shirt pressed and ready to go. "How do you do that?"

"It's called being a bachelor and being too poor to afford dry cleaning." Daniel grinned and held out the shirt, then waited while Nick slipped it on. Then he unplugged the iron and set it on the ironing board to cool. "And *I'm* not distracted by thoughts of a woman right now."

"I'm not distracted."

Daniel arched a brow.

"Okay, maybe I am. A little." Nick picked up his keys, slid them into his pocket, then faced his brother. "I thought I was over her. Over the whole damned thing. Then I see her last night at the toy store and—"

"It was *Love Story* all over again?" Daniel hummed a snippet of the movie's famous theme song.

"Not at all. More a remake of our worst moments together." But there had been one moment when he'd remembered why he'd been attracted to her. Why he'd married her. They'd had fun—for a few minutes—and then Carolyn had gone back to being the stuffy city prosecutor, the woman who was about as much fun as a bag of rocks, and Nick was reminded all over again why they'd broken up.

Yet guilt pinged at him still. She hadn't been the only one at fault, and he knew it. He hadn't exactly been Joe Sensitive, nor had he been Husband of the Year.

"I'm just glad I got out of that marriage after a few days instead of a few years," Nick said. "Carolyn was always too damned straight-laced for me. I want a woman who can have a good time, make me laugh, live a little. Not drive me absolutely insane. And when I think of Carolyn Duff, driving me crazy is the term that comes to mind."

Daniel bent down to pat Bandit, Nick's German short-haired pointer. The spotted dog wagged his tail with furious joy, nearly knocking over the scraggly ficus tree beside him. A shower of dry leaves littered the floor. "There were some good times, too, from what you've told me. Some *very* good times."

An image of one particularly good memory—with the neon lights of Vegas shining on Carolyn's peach skin while they made use of every surface in their suite at the Mirage—flashed in Nick's mind. He saw her smile, heard her laughter, could almost smell the scent of her raspberry bubble bath.

"Okay, maybe one good memory. Or two." Another one popped into his mind, followed quickly by a third, slamming with a sting like pellets into his chest. Nick shook his head. As good as those times had been, the end had been fast and unforeseen, like a sneak guerrilla attack that came and ripped him apart in the middle of the night.

Carolyn had been stubborn about leaving him in that diner, adamant about ending the marriage as fast as it began, claiming he hadn't cared, he hadn't been listening.

And back then he probably hadn't. But she hadn't given him much of a chance, either.

Just as well. They'd been totally unsuited for each other.

Since the day of the divorce, Nick and Caroline had become nothing more than strangers, albeit strangers who had once shared a bed. And yet last night he'd sensed a vulnerability in her, a chink in the Carolyn armor, that made the lawyer in him see a flicker of doubt in the witness's case.

He wondered—could he have been wrong in letting her go? Could they make it work if they tried again now?

Nick shook his head. He hadn't changed much in three years, and from what he'd seen, neither had she. "We were insane to get married in the first place," he said to Daniel. *Definitely insane.*

Still, at odd moments, Nick thought the exact opposite. Crazy thoughts, the kind that hit him in the middle of the night when he awoke from a dream that had featured a lot of neon lights and left him pacing the floors. He'd raid the fridge or pour a scotch, and still the memories would tickle at the edges of his mind.

He was a lawyer. Even though he'd had a lot of evidence, and a whole lot of facts in the case of his marriage, he knew when someone was hiding the truth. Carolyn most definitely had been keeping a tidbit or two in check when she'd handed back the plain gold band, sliding it across the table of the diner, then walked out of his life.

Until yesterday.

Nick shrugged it off. They were totally different people—and they were over. Two very good reasons to put Carolyn out of his mind.

Daniel straightened. Bandit let out a whine of complaint, then trotted off to find a toy for fetch. "Maybe this wasn't just serendipity, you two running into each other. Both of you getting kids to sponsor for that picnic thing. Maybe it was a sign from the Fates or whatever."

"Will you let it go?"

"Only if you tell me what made you two start talking to each other after all this time apart."

"Desperation." Nick chuckled. "We were both stuck in the toy aisle, me with a girl to buy for, her with a boy, and we didn't know what we were doing. Forced allies, nothing more."

"Uh-huh. You couldn't have asked any of the moms there? Or called your sisters?" Daniel said. "All of whom would have willingly given you advice."

"I, ah, didn't think of that."

"Told you. You were blinded by the pretty woman who still gets your car engine racing."

Nick rolled his eyes. "If you weren't my brother, I would stop talking to you. I've told you a thousand times that Carolyn and I aren't any good together. You know that old adage about the bird and the fish?" Daniel nodded. "Well, try imagining that same fable with a hawk and a shark."

"With you being the shark, I presume?" His brother gave him a good-natured jab in the arm. "Corporate lawyers, you're all the same."

"Hey, I take offense to that. You know I'm not like other lawyers. I'm more…unconventional. Fun."

"You're looking pretty conventional right now." Daniel gave his older brother's pressed golf shirt a light pat. Bandit took the opportunity to bound over and deposit an orange plastic bone at Daniel's feet.

"Oh, but I'm still unconventional underneath." Nick raised the left sleeve, baring his arm and the tattoo he'd had for the last three years. The still-vivid image of a cartoon shark—a joke he'd had put on his arm back in law school—never showed under Nick's suits, but usually peeked out from under the hem of his short-sleeved shirts.

"Of course. I expected nothing less. And I still think that's the most apropos image for you, big brother. You do realize, though, that both hawks and sharks are predators? That puts you two in the same class of animal." Daniel grinned, then tossed the bone down the hall. Bandit took off after it, running too fast and skidding past the vinyl squeaky toy before scrambling back around to snatch it up. "So what are you going to drive this time? What was it for the senior prom? A backhoe? Took out a damned tree on your way home, I might add."

"It was a tractor. My date about died, but no one forgot my entrance." Nick took the toy from Bandit, repeating the same scramble, miss and skid pattern as before. "That dog never learns."

"Neither do you," Daniel pointed out. "You're still as crazy as when we were kids. Sending your assistant on an impromptu trip to Jamaica—"

"To boost office morale."

Daniel went on, ignoring Nick's interruption. "Karaoke singing, without the musical accompaniment—"

"Just having fun."

"In *court*?"

Nick shrugged, pleading no contest to the charges. "I won the case, I might add. Proved my client's jingle was not offensive."

"And hosting a birthday party for your nephew, complete with pony rides and a petting zoo in your backyard, for God's sake. You know that you about made our sister have a heart attack. She is not the pony ride type." Daniel shook his head. "It's like you thrive on fun."

Daniel was right. He did indeed thrive on having fun. After growing up in a hectic family, fun was what he knew. It was as familiar as his own face, and it gave him an odd sense of comfort. And it helped him feel like he hadn't become too much of a grown-up yet.

But lately it had grown tired. He had a house—an investment property—but it was empty, except for Monday nights when his friends came over to watch the game. He'd dated women who laughed, women who were…fun. But not serious.

Carolyn Duff had been serious. The one serious girl on the Lawford U campus. So serious she'd offered a challenge, an exciting allure to Nick, who'd set out to make her smile, laugh. After their first date he'd found something in her he hadn't found in other women, a depth of character that made him want to try harder. Be more than he had been up until then. She'd brought a sober touch to his life, the kind that had him toying with the idea of settling down, becoming a grown-up. And so he'd had that crazy idea of running off to Vegas and getting married.

Because he'd thought he could have it all.

But no.

Nick swallowed the bitter taste of disappointment. He was happier this way anyway. Unencumbered. Free. Answering to no one's drum but his own.

He slid the directions to the picnic into his pocket, then checked again to be sure he had his keys and wallet, along with a deck of cards. "Well, I'm not doing anything like that today. I've had enough surprises for a while."

Daniel walked with his brother to the door and waited while Nick locked up, leaving a dejected Bandit inside. "Where you and Carolyn are concerned, I think the surprises are just starting."

"No, we're over. Have been since she dumped me on the drive home from Vegas three years ago."

"Uh-huh," Daniel said, clearly not believing a word. "I'll believe that when I see you two together and there's no more electricity between you than two clods of dirt. Remember the day I stopped by for lunch last year? I saw the two of you in the hallway of the courtroom. I'm lucky I'm still alive."

"What do you mean, still alive?"

Daniel clutched his heart and faked gagging. "The way you two looked at each other, it was like a couple of light sabers going at it. She wants you. You want her. If the math was any simpler, it would be preschool."

"You forget everything else that goes into that equation. Like the fact that she ditched me to go off and put herself into the middle of a hostage situation, even after I begged her not to. That she also realized she didn't have time for a marriage, not that and a career, too. That this had all been some crazy impromptu decision she made and just wanted to forget. Like buying a pair of shoes that didn't match her dress."

Daniel chuckled. "Aren't we the jaded one?"

"Come talk to me when you make a commitment to something other than a car lease."

Daniel raised his hands in surrender. The two men headed down the stairs of Nick's front porch and paused at the end of the walkway. The July sun had already raised the temperature to the mid eighties, making Nick glad he'd opted for light khaki shorts to wear with the cream shirt. The event organizers had put "casual attire" on the invitations, not "business," and for that, Nick was grateful. There was nothing worse than standing around all day in the heat in a suit.

"So, you're still claiming you have no interest in her?" Daniel asked.

Nick shook his head. "There's nothing between us. Not anymore."

Daniel tick-tocked a finger at him. "Don't lie to me, big brother. I grew up with you, remember? I know the signs of you getting ready for a date."

"It's a benefit picnic. For needy children."

Daniel laughed. "And the children really needed you to wear cologne, trim your nails and press your shirt?"

"I wanted to look…" Nick cut himself off before he said the word *good*, which would imply that he cared what Carolyn thought of his appearance. And he didn't care. At all. "Professional."

"Let's see how 'professional' Carolyn looks in your eyes today." Daniel winked. "And like I said, how long the two of you resist each other."

Carolyn sat at a picnic table on the fairgrounds of the Lawford City Park, surrounded by busy, chattering children, and did her best to keep her gaze off the park's gaily decorated entrance and on the task at hand. The problem was, she wasn't very good at either.

She'd bought a new dress—darn Mary and her suggestion—just that morning. She shifted on the bench, acutely aware of the bright-blue-and-white dress and how she had gone to an awful lot of work on her appearance for something that was supposed to be casual.

"Geez, Miss Duff, can't you make an eagle?" a little girl with a name tag that read Kimberly asked. "I learned how to make birds in kindergarten."

Carolyn cursed whoever had come up with the craft for this table. A bald eagle paper bag puppet, AKA a torture marathon with paper. There were wings and talons and a beak to make. Little pieces of construction paper to glue all over the place. One side had to be the front, and Lord forgive if she got it wrong because then, apparently, the eagle couldn't eat.

The kids had already informed her, with a look

of disdain, that her first eagle attempt would have died of starvation. So now Carolyn was making her second lunch bag bird.

And clearly mangling the thing into a version of roadkill. "There aren't any rules decreeing we *have* to make an American eagle. What about a Monarch butterfly? Or a nice little robin?" She gave Kimberly an encouraging, work-with-me smile.

Kimberly returned a blank stare. "Isn't this a birthday party for *our* country? And isn't the eagle our country's bird?"

The kid had her there. Darn, these third-graders were awfully smart.

This was one more reason why Carolyn hadn't had children. Because she wouldn't know what on earth to do with one after delivery. Why she'd been assigned to this table, she'd never know. It had to be one of Mary's brainstorms.

Speaking of whom, Mary waved to her from across the field. Carolyn gave her a grimace back. Mary either didn't see the facial gesture or chose to ignore it. She just went back to blithely setting up the food. The younger children were attending a puppet show put on by a local bookstore. The performance was due to end any second and thus the children would be arriving soon. Then the rest of the festivities would get underway. The third-graders at Carolyn's table had pronounced them-

selves too "old" for such a babyish activity, so
Carolyn had been asked to oversee them and keep
them busy in the meantime.

A flutter of nerves ran through Carolyn at the
thought of meeting her sponsored child. She chided
herself. She was an attorney. She'd faced down
threatening criminals. Blustering defense attorneys.
Stern-faced judges. She shouldn't be nervous about
meeting a five-year-old, for Pete's sake.

"Uh, Kimberly, let's forget the eagle. And create
another display of patriotism." Carolyn crumpled
the lunch bag into a ball and reached into the craft
bucket for new supplies. "Here we are, children.
Flags. The perfect Fourth of July symbol." She
handed each child squares of red, white and blue
paper, then cut out red strips. This she could do.
She hoped. Carolyn began gluing, drizzling the
white Elmer's along the edge of the red strips,
then laying them on top of the white squares. The
glue smeared out from under the red strips, turning
it into a messy puddle, dampening the construction paper and turning the tips of her fingers pink.

Kimberly, who had already completed a flag
and whose paper was neat and nearly perfect, just
shook her head.

Carolyn sighed. Too much glue. Geez, what
had she been doing during her childhood years?
She'd forgotten the simplest of crafts. And then

she remembered why with a pang in her chest. She knew the exact minute she stopped being a little girl and turned into a grown-up.

The day she'd watched her father die. No, not die—he'd been murdered. Shot right in front of her.

Because he'd sacrificed himself for her.

The memory sliced through Carolyn with a sharp ache, like a break that had never healed properly. She drew in a breath, sucked the pain back to the recesses of her mind. Carolyn had lost her father, lost her entire world, and been sent to live with her aunt Greta, who didn't believe in bringing children up with tea parties and construction paper, but with discipline and hard work.

She'd been nine, probably the same age as the kids around her. And much too young, she knew now, to quit working with construction paper.

Carolyn shook off the maudlin thoughts and returned her attention to the half-dozen kids and the stacks of red, white and blue paper. The children were all busily making their versions of Fourth of July festivity, seemingly unaware that many of them lived with families whose income fell in the shadows of poverty level. Hence, the benefit picnic. For the kids, at least, Carolyn would do her best and make a flag.

Oh, for Pete's sake. A flag was about as simple as crafts got. Then one glance at the crumpled roadkill eagle project reminded Carolyn looks could be deceiving, particularly when there was craft glue involved.

"I've passed the bar exam. I can do this," she muttered. She wasn't going to let a third-grader show her up. She'd do this—and do it even cooler than her young charges.

And it would keep her mind off expecting to see Nick at any moment. If she was lucky, he'd just drop off the toys and skip the main event, especially after their earlier exchange at the toy store.

Carolyn reached into the center of the table, grabbed a ruler and a fresh sheet of red paper, traced exact lines from corner to corner, then cut out new stripes. Kimberly watched her for a second, then elbowed the other little girl beside her, Veronica, according to her name tag. The two of them stopped their flag construction to watch as Carolyn measured a perfect rectangle of white, then carefully applied dots of glue to her stripes, marked their placement with the ruler and affixed them.

"My teacher would like your flag," said a little boy with tousled brown hair. His name tag, placed upside down on his chest, read Paul. "She likes everything neat. I'm messy." He held up his flag, which looked so much like Carolyn's first attempt, it was embarrassing.

"She's getting better," Kimberly said to Veronica.

"At least this one doesn't look dead." Veronica pointed at Carolyn's first beakless eagle.

Carolyn didn't spare her peanut gallery a look. She simply went on with her project, adding a perfect square of blue to the upper left corner. Kimberly slipped her the packet of silver stars. "Thank you," Carolyn said.

"There should be fifty of them, in case you didn't know. I know because Miss Laramie told me. She's really smart."

"And I can see that you are quite intelligent, too," Carolyn said.

Kimberly beamed.

Carolyn withdrew the first stars from the packet and was about to stick them on when she realized exactly why Mary had sat her at this table. So Carolyn could interact with the children.

Work with them.

Get to know them.

Duh. She'd done about as much interacting as a potted plant. She probably had more experience with philodendrons, too. Once again, Carolyn slapped on a smile. "Kimberly, Veronica. Would you two assist me in affixing the stars?" Carolyn gestured toward the pile of shiny five-pointers. "And then Paul can finish the task?"

"What's 'affix'?" Veronica asked. "Is that like a kind of glue?"

"I think it's a color," Paul suggested. "Isn't it?" He gave Carolyn a confused look, then worried his lower lip.

"*Affix* means to fasten, to attach," Carolyn explained, then noticed she was still surrounded by blank looks. "Yes, glue."

"Uh, Miss Duff, those are stickers," Veronica said, then peeled off the paper backing and stuck one of the stars on her flag. "See?"

"Oh. Of course. Well, will you help me stick them on, then? Please?"

At that, the girls brightened. They dug into the package and started slapping them onto the blue square, not in the neat rows that Carolyn would have preferred, but in a slipshod fashion that soon took the shape of a flower. Carolyn smiled and praised their creativity, telling herself that she was here to relax, not become an anal-retentive craft woman.

And as Paul added his stars at the bottom, forming "grass" for the flower, Carolyn had to admit the new version of the flag was cute. Different. A true melting pot of other people. "This is perfect," she told the kids. "You've managed to capture the spirit of democracy in America. Excellent attention to detail."

The kids just blinked, jaws slack.

"I see you've managed to make some friends," said a familiar voice.

Nick.

Carolyn turned around, trying to stay aloof, cool as an ice cube. Not an easy feat, considering Nick managed to look both handsome and boyish in shorts and a golf shirt.

Then she caught a glimpse of his tattoo, peeking out from under the sleeve of his light cream-colored shirt and a hit of desire slammed into her so hard, she had to hold her breath to keep from betraying the feeling. He still had it. Well, of course he would. A tattoo was a permanent kind of thing.

The memory careened through her mind. Meeting him that first day, her gaze sliding to that left arm, seeing the unconventional, unexpected adornment on his upper arm, and immediately being intrigued. Attracted. After his magic trick, they'd talked, and she'd done something she'd never done before—

Asked him out on a date, a date that had lasted long into the next day. Not because they'd slept together, but because they hadn't stopped talking. For days they'd talked, about everything under the sun. In him she'd found someone so different, so open, she'd become a human conversational waterfall. Three weeks later they'd been married.

Four days later, divorced.

And three years later, she still couldn't forget

him. Or that tattoo. "Here to join in on the crafts, Mr. Gilbert?"

"Uh…no. I'm not exactly crafter material." He glanced at the table of children, now arguing over the supply of scissors and paper. "Besides, I think you have it under control."

Carolyn laughed. "That's an illusion."

He cleared his throat. "Actually, I came over to see if you'd seen Mary yet. I know the younger children are due to arrive soon and I was looking forward to meeting Angela."

Why did disappointment ripple through her when he didn't mention anything about seeing her? Noticing her dress? That she'd left her hair down, instead of putting it back into her usual chignon? She didn't want Nick to be interested in her again. She didn't want to relive her past. "Mary was over at the food table, last I saw her."

Instead of glancing in that direction, Nick considered Carolyn for a long second. She felt as if he could see past every wall she'd constructed, every bit of armor she'd put in place over the years.

He leaned down, until his mouth met her ear, his breath whispered past a lock of her hair. "You look beautiful today, Carolyn."

Something hot and warm raced through her veins. She refused to react to him, though her hormones didn't seem to be riding the same resolve wagon.

"Thank you."

He was still close, so close she could see the flecks of gold in his eyes. If she leaned a few inches to the right, she could touch him. Feel his cheek against hers.

"Oooh, Miss Duff has a boyfriend," Veronica sing-songed. "Miss Duff and Mr. Stranger, up in a tree—"

"*K-I-S-S-I-N-G,*" joined in a chorus of young voices.

What were they teaching these kids in school nowadays? A lot more than reading and writing, that was for sure. Carolyn turned her Evil Eye on the group, the one parenting trick she'd learned from her aunt. "We're just colleagues. And we're *not* kissing."

Not now. Not later. Not ever again.

"I thought a collie was a dog," Paul said, his face scrunched up in confusion.

"It is, Paul." Nick slipped onto the wooden bench and took a seat beside Carolyn. "Now, what are you making here?"

"A flag."

"A flag, huh? Cool." He glanced at Carolyn. The tension of the day knotted her shoulders, surely showed in her face. Nick gave her a grin— the grin that said he had read her and her unease with both her charges and the task as easily as the newspaper—then turned back to the kids. "You want to know what else is cool?" He withdrew a deck of cards from his pocket, slid them out of the box and laid the stack on the table. "Who wants to see a little magic?" All three kids raised their hands. But Nick turned to her. He held her gaze for a split second, long enough to communicate that it would all work out, if she would just trust him. "Miss Duff, do you want to do the honors and pick a card?" He pushed the deck in front of her.

Just trust him.

Carolyn hesitated. She glanced at the kids. They stared at her. Her stomach clenched, and she looked back at Nick, suddenly terrified he'd leave her alone with them and more of those stupid paper-bag eagles. "Okay, Nick," she said, then she reached forward, cut the deck and picked one of the red-backed cards. She showed the three of diamonds to the children, keeping it from Nick's view. Then she slipped it back into the deck.

Paul's eyes were wide with excitement. "Oh, did you see that card? It was the—"

"No, don't tell me," Nick said, putting up a finger. "I'm going to read Carolyn's mind and tell all of you what her card is." He squeezed his eyes shut, making a big production out of the whole trick. He put out a hand, touched his fingertips to Carolyn's forehead. "I'm seeing…something red."

Veronica and Kimberly gasped. Carolyn smiled. Paul's jaw dropped.

"And in diamonds."

The kids looked at each other, shock and awe written all over their features. Carolyn kept a bemused smile on her face, giving nothing away. This was Nick at his best, taking center stage, working a group, creating his magic.

Nick pretended to concentrate more, his fingers fluttering over Carolyn's face. He drew back, opened his eyes. "Is your card…the three of diamonds?"

The kids exploded in wonder. "How did you know that?"

"That's cool!"

"Oh, my goodness! He really does know magic!"

And just like that, Nick had the children at Carolyn's table chattering with him, laughing and showing off their flags and eagles. He marveled over each one like they were the next Picasso. In an instant he'd accumulated a Nick fan club. And Carolyn, who hadn't managed any of that, was left feeling like the lunchroom lady dispensing the broccoli.

On the other side of the park, a big yellow bus pulled up, announcing the arrival of the younger children. Mary signaled to Nick and Carolyn. "You ready?" Nick asked.

"Sure." Though she felt anything but. Her success rate thus far had been zero.

Nick laid a hand on hers. "I'm sure you and Bobby are going to get along just fine."

Nevertheless, a quiver of doubt rose in her stomach. As the other children dispersed to find their sponsors, Carolyn rose to clean up the mess on the table. Before she could protest, she found Nick by her side, helping. She scooped the scraps of paper into a nearby trash bag. Nick did the same, and for an instant his hand brushed against hers.

A surge of want rushed through her, as if she'd been denied water for a month and had just come into contact with a pool of it. It was only because she hadn't touched him in three years. That was all.

Damn that Nick Gilbert. Being around him was always like this—distracting, crazy.

He made her forget. Forget her priorities. Forget what was important. And most of all, forget that when she needed him, he wouldn't be there.

If there was one thing Aunt Greta had drilled into Carolyn's head, it was this: Losing focus created mistakes. And mistakes led to people getting hurt, to losing the ones you loved. It led to showdowns in convenience stores, with men who should have been behind bars instead of holding guns to people's heads.

No. She wouldn't get involved with Nick. Not again.

Carolyn yanked her hand back, opting to stack the pile of scissors instead. If she were smart, she'd poke Nick with one and make him go away. But in a park full of lawyers, assault with a cutting implement probably wasn't a good idea.

"Carolyn…"

The way he said her name, in the same soft, hushed tone he'd used years before, made her pause. She didn't move, didn't turn around. Didn't look in those blue eyes. Because she knew if she did she'd be a goner. "What?"

"Today will go just fine. You'll be okay."

The man knew her too well. Knew her past. Knew her secrets. And that gave him an unfair advantage that choked her throat.

Carolyn finished clearing the table, avoiding his gaze. She loaded the containers into her arms and turned to face him. "Of course it will. And for you, too. Enjoy your day, Nick."

The temperature between them dropped.

"You as well, Miss Duff." Then he turned on his heel and walked away.

The bus carrying the younger children emptied out, spilling children into the park like water emptying from a pitcher. In a second Bobby would be here. Carolyn would give him the presents, they'd eat lunch and then the picnic would end. Nick would go home and so would Carolyn, their temporary association over. Just as well.

She knew she'd made the right choice, then and now. Nick was spontaneity personified; she was the one who stayed on the straight and narrow path. She'd learned that was where her talents lay—working in an environment she could control. Predict. Reason with. It was how she had survived her childhood after her father died. It was what she knew and understood, a world as comfortable as a blanket.

Nick Gilbert, on the other hand, she couldn't predict. Control. Or reason with. And that was exactly why she was going to make sure everything about him stayed in the past—as soon as this day was over.

CHAPTER FOUR

NICK lost the staring contest before it barely began.

"Okay, so I've done this before," Angela began, her green eyes assessing him. "And you don't have to, like, hang out with me or even pretend to be nice. I know you're just here because you have to be."

Nick bit back a grin. "Same as you, right?"

She nodded. "Exactly."

He put out his hand, waited for her to put her much smaller one into his and shake on it. "We're agreed. Not to be friends, just—"

"Stuck together. Until another Madeline thing is over and I go back to the fosters."

Nick released Angela's hand, then gestured toward a bench beside the playground. Children climbed in and out of the brightly painted equipment, laughing and happy, while the sponsors stood around in little chatting clusters with foster parents and real parents. Angela, however, acted as if she was years and years beyond such games.

How sad, Nick thought. Sadder than anything he'd seen in a long time. He didn't have much experience with kids, heck, any experience besides his brothers and sisters and their children, but even he knew this wasn't what kids should sound like. Jaded. Bitter. Like they could care less.

"Okay, *I'm* new at this, so you'll have to translate. Madeline thing? Fosters?"

Angela rolled her eyes. "You know *Madeline,* the book? The one that makes being an orphan look like one big adventure?"

That struck a memory in him of something he'd read as a kid. "Oh, that one. Full of nice nuns and cute dogs."

"Exactly." Angela nodded. "Except real orphanages aren't like that."

"I'm sorry."

Angela picked at an invisible piece of lint on her denim shorts. They were clean but worn, and Nick wondered if they were hand-me-downs. From an older child in the family where she was staying? From another foster child? From her old life? "The fosters aren't so bad," Angela said. "Most of 'em."

"Your foster parents."

She nodded. Her blond curls bounced with the movement, framing her face in a light halo that reflected the sun in a golden cloud. "These ones are kind of nice. Better than the ones before."

Nick didn't want to ask about "the ones before." Those five words were enough to tell him that this girl had been through more in her six years on earth than he had been in his twenty-eight. Suddenly he wanted to draw her against him and promise nothing bad would ever happen to her again.

But he couldn't. So he didn't.

"Are you happy there?" Nick asked. This was an odd position for him, being a sort of pseudoparent, even on a temporary basis. He wasn't used to being the grown-up, at least being any more grown-up than he had to be in the courtroom, and it forced him to think in new ways. Forced him to look at the world differently than he ever had before.

To see a world outside the two-parent, mostly ideal one he'd grown up in, too.

"Yeah." Angela shrugged. "The fosters say they want to adopt me." She pointed toward a tall, friendly looking couple across the park, who looked as if they had stepped out of a magazine for perfect parents. They waved and smiled at Angela. Nice, happy, trying to include her in the family. "I'm waiting. See what they do."

Hedging her bets, Nick was sure. Not committing her heart until the ink was dry. He saw a flicker of hope in Angela's eyes, then she popped off the bench, smoothed her shorts again.

"I can go play with the other kids, and you can

go with *them*, if you want." She gestured at the other lawyers.

Nick looked down into Angela's eyes and thought he'd never seen anyone look as lonely and in need of a friend as she did. He could do "friend." "Parent"…probably not so well. "Nope. I'm fine right here. I'll let you in on a secret. Lawyers are totally not fun. And they don't know any good jokes."

A smile flitted across her face, then blew away like a candle in a windstorm. She shrugged. "Okay, whatever."

A tough cookie, this one.

Nick reached into his pocket and pulled out a quarter. "Do you believe in magic, Angela?"

She eyed him. "Not really. It's for little kids." But he could see a part of her still really wanted to be a little kid.

And that, at least, Nick could give her. He was good at that.

As Nick bent down and began working magic with a quarter and swift fingers, making the coin disappear and reappear in Angela's ear, behind her head, under her chin—every time eliciting a smile and a gasp of surprise from the girl who'd given up on magic—Nick's gaze strayed across the park to Carolyn. Even from here he could see her stiff posture, the frustration on her face as she struggled to connect with Bobby, her sponsored child.

And he realized he had, indeed, seen that look of loneliness and of being lost, in another's eyes once before—and noticed it lingered still, all these years later.

Once before, he'd taken on the challenge of getting her to loosen up, and had had fun winning his own personal bet. Could he do it a second time? This time, not with the intention of winning her back—he'd already been down that road and knew where it led—but to help her make some inroads with those kids today. He didn't know who looked more uncomfortable—Carolyn or poor Bobby.

But as Nick crossed the field toward the table, one nagging doubt in his chest told him this time around getting past those walls Carolyn Duff had in place was going to take more than a simple magic trick.

He came up behind her, so quietly she almost didn't notice. But Carolyn knew Nick could have been as silent as the wind and still she would have sensed his presence, felt him there.

"Do you need some help?" he said.

Did she need help? She needed an army battalion of it. Carolyn hadn't felt so over her head since she'd prosecuted her first criminal case alone. Bobby Lester had stopped talking after exchanging a total of three words with her—"hi" and "thank you." She'd earned a few smiles for the gifts, which had let her know she'd at least made good shopping choices, thanks to Nick's advice, but the boy was as closemouthed as a clam. Now, he was off eating lunch with the other children, which was supposed to be followed by a short film in the park's pavilion. Carolyn had volunteered to set up the games. Anything to avoid another trip into a conversational No Man's Land. "No, I'm fine."

"And elephants are parading in the sky today, too." Nick put a hand on her shoulder, the touch searing through the light cotton of her dress, and turned her gently to face him. "It's not such a bad thing to ask for help, Carolyn."

"Really, Nick, this thing with the kids, it's nothing. A few games with some children." Children who wouldn't talk to her. Children who were as foreign to her as Martians.

She could do this. Heck, she could command a courtroom. Could get the toughest criminals to confess. Could win over the most jaded juries. So what if she had all the homemaking skills of a monkey?

"Why won't you let me help you?" he said. "Or let me get someone to—"

"I can handle this, Nick."

Frustration sparked in his eyes and he took a step back. "Of course. I forgot. You're Carolyn Duff, the bulldog who works alone. Doesn't need anyone."

She pivoted away from him. "Don't…don't call me that. It sounds…" The words trailed off, caught in her throat.

"Sounds what?"

"Sounds so cold coming from you." The nickname she had taken pride in because it meant she was doing her job—the very job that had broken them apart.

"How about if I call you Carolyn the Yorkie pup?" A tease in Nick's voice, erasing all offense.

She laughed. "Marginally better."

He moved closer. Every ounce of her went on alert, even though they were still a very respectable distance apart. "You're not okay. I can tell."

"I am."

"You couldn't lie if your life depended on it, Counselor."

"Then it's a good thing I'm not on the witness stand."

He watched her, his gaze sweeping over her features. "How have you been, Carolyn? *Really* been since we broke up?"

She started to say fine, but before she could

get a word out, Nick interrupted her with another question.

"Do you still sleep with the lights on?" he asked, his voice quiet, concerned.

One question. That's all it took to remind her that ninety-nine percent of the time, her life was completely in control. That everything was exactly as she wanted it. But there was that one percent that once in a while—when night fell—remembered a moment in her past that had turned everything from wonderful to terrible.

She swallowed, but her throat remained parched. "He's in jail, Nick. It's over. And I'm fine." She turned back to the games, getting to work. Stay busy, stay on task. Stay organized—and stay away from Nick. Who, even if she had told him all the details of her past, had never really listened. Not really.

"Well, if you need to talk, I'm here, you know. We're still friends."

She wheeled back to face him. "Come on, Nick. We're not anything anymore. And if I needed someone to talk to, it wouldn't be you."

He let out a gust. "Why not me?"

"You don't take anything seriously. That was half the problem. And that's fine, that's who you are. Makes you good with kids, at parties, not so good with relationships. So stop trying to perform an instant therapy session at a picnic, Nick. Just let it go." She moved away, inserting distance. As much distance as she could, with the intensifying heat, the baking sun, the fenced-in area where all the games would be held, all of it seeming so much more enclosed with Nick here.

She cast a glance in the direction of the pavilion, but the children were all sitting on blankets, watching a mermaid dance and sing on a projection screen. No saved-by-the-bell help to distract Nick would be arriving anytime soon. "I don't have time for this, anyway. I have to get these games set up. The kids will be done anytime now, and if we don't keep them entertained they'll run rampant, and you know that will just drive Mary crazy. Just imagine a whole slew of little ones…" Carolyn kept rambling as she laid out rows of bean bags for the tic-tac-toe toss, then reached for a series of bright rainbow-colored beach balls and yellow plastic bats. "…and if we're not ready, they'll just run roughshod over—"

"Hey, don't be the game martyr here, Carolyn," Nick said, interrupting her, laying a hand on hers, taking some of the toys out of her grasp. "Let me help."

"I've got it under control."

"Of course you do," Nick said, then ignored her completely, moving down to the next set of games and reaching into the boxes to set up the fishing poles and magnetic fish that went along with the six-foot, round plastic pool that had been filled earlier. "Didn't you just say, though, that I'm the one who excels at games? Let the master be of assistance."

She may be the one with the nickname of bulldog, but she knew she wasn't the only one with the canine's famous tenacity. What if Nick had been like that about their marriage? What if he had fought that hard to hold on to her? To get to know her, really know her. Not just play at being married, like it was a game of fetch.

But he hadn't. He had argued with her that day, of course, but then he had signed the papers and let her go, never saying another word.

He'd given up on them as quickly as a man giving up on a sport he couldn't master. A part of her had been relieved, and a part of her had been disappointed. Heartbroken.

Realizing that Nick may have spoken a good game about wanting her, loving her to no end—

And then in reality, not really meaning any of it. He'd done what Nick did best—chased her until he had the prize, then let her down when she needed him most.

Carolyn spun around, the beanbags rustling in her grasp. "Why are you *really* here, Nick?"

He paused. "Same as you. I sponsored a child,

so I'm doing my part. Delivering the toys, inter-acting with my sponsoree."

"No, I meant here with me. You can interact at the food table. The craft table. A million places other than here. You really don't need to help me…or keep trying to prove whatever point you are trying to prove."

"Here come the kids," he said.

And indeed Nick was saved from answering by a rising tide of excited voices, their high-pitched squeals coming at Nick and Carolyn like a chorus of dolphins.

"Brace yourself," Nick whispered in Carolyn's ear, so close, so very close. And her resolve to stay away from him weakened.

Just a bit.

"Nick!" A little girl barreled forward, out of the crowd, straight into Nick's legs, the force of her greeting breaking Nick and Carolyn apart. The little girl clasped him tight. With a laugh, Nick reached down and swung her up, into his arms.

"Hey, Angela. Did you have fun?"

She nodded. "Uh-huh. Did I tell you about the movie we saw after lunch? It was a mermaid movie. I love mermaid movies. Especially mermaid movies with lots of fish. I love fish. 'Cuz I love to swim. Except I've never had a pool. I really wish I had a pool. Do you have a pool?"

"Nope. But I like to swim, too. Swimming's pretty fun, especially when there's a slide or a diving board involved."

Carolyn scanned the crowd, seeking the face of Bobby. All the while, she listened to the excited chatter of Angela and Nick's enthusiastic responses. How had he done that? Struck up such an immediate rapport with the child?

"Hi, Miss Duff."

Carolyn looked down. Bobby stood before her, as solemn as a judge about to sentence a serial killer. "Hello, Bobby. Was your excursion entertaining?"

"Uh-huh."

"And the film? Did you find that enjoyable?"

Bobby toed at the grass. "Uh-huh."

Carolyn scrambled for another subject, something, anything. "Wonderful. Is that because you enjoy films with mermaids?"

Bobby's face scrunched up, and his shoulders rose and dropped. "They're girls."

Carolyn took that as a negative. Okay. So she'd asked all the same questions Nick had, and received four words in response. None of the instantaneous best-buds stuff. What was she doing wrong?

"We've been instructed to pair up for the games," Carolyn said to the boy, indicating the first race, where other volunteers had slipped into place to man the stations. "Would you like to be on my team? For potato-sack races and the bean-bag toss?"

Bobby glanced up at her, dubious. "Miss Duff, you're a…"

"A what?" Carolyn prompted when he didn't finish.

"A girl. I don't know if you'd be a good racer."

"I ran track in high school, Bobby. I assure you, I'd be a wonderful racer." Since Carolyn hadn't done anything like this in what felt like a thousand years, she couldn't be really sure. And her experience with children was nil, so her comfort level was in the negative digits. Still she put on a bright smile. "What do you say, want to give it a shot?"

Bobby gave her a look that said he'd rather be sentenced to a lifetime of community service. "Do I have to? Can I just sit on the bench over there? And watch?"

"Oh, yes. Certainly." Carolyn watched him go, trying not to feel like a complete and total failure.

She was surrounded by laughing, happy pairings. Sponsors and children who were slipping legs into potato sacks, talking as if they'd known each other for years. And here she couldn't get one five-year-old to think she had any game ability at all.

"Seems you're one leg short of a sack race."

Nick's voice. Carolyn turned around, to find

Nick and Angela behind her. For a moment, she considered not admitting the truth, then decided that if she didn't get some help with this kid thing, Bobby's entire day would be a bust. And the most important thing here was Bobby—not her pride. "I lost my partner. He doesn't find me very… fun," she said, lowering her voice, "because I'm a girl."

Nick chuckled. "Now *that* I understand, being the older brother of some not-so-fun sisters."

"Girls can be fun. I'm…fun."

"You are." A smile curved up his face. "Or at least, you were. From what I remember."

A heat brewed between them, built on past memories, but Carolyn knew they were as fragile as tissues, and nothing to build a future on. She brushed it off. "Well, apparently, Bobby doesn't agree."

"Want to trade, for the race? Angela won't mind, I'm sure. Once she came out of her shell and began to trust me, she really opened up. She's a great sport."

"Nick, I'm not so good at this kind of thing." Carolyn shifted from foot to foot, suddenly uncomfortable with the whole idea of racing in a sack in front of her colleagues. Possibly falling on her face. Making a fool of herself. Carolyn the Bulldog losing control, being silly? So not her. "I should probably sit out the games and—"

"How will you ever get good at being with kids if you don't try?"

"And why would I want to get good at being with kids?"

"Because someday, Miss Duff, you might just want to try marriage again." His gaze met hers, and something hot and dark burned in their depths, something she couldn't read. "There may be a man who captures your heart. A man you want to stay with. A man you want to make a future with. So why not take a taste of the future today?"

"Because—" She cut off the sentence. She couldn't finish it, not here. Not in front of all these people. That was a little more information than the entire Lawford legal community needed to hear.

And besides, the days when she told Nick Gilbert her plans for her romantic future were way in the past.

"Angela," Nick said, waving the little girl over. "I want you to meet a friend of mine."

Angela bopped across the grass, her blond curls springing up and down with her steps. She beamed up at Carolyn. "Hello. I'm Angela."

"This is Carolyn," Nick said.

"Miss Duff," Carolyn corrected.

"Miss Duff?" Nick arched a brow.

"Well, children should learn to be respectful. And formal. If boundaries aren't put in place—"

"For Pete's sake, Carolyn, this is supposed to be a casual event. And we're making friends here, aren't we, Angela?" He bent down and smiled at the girl. She nodded, curls bouncing like they were on a moonwalk. "Friends go by first names."

"But—"

"This isn't a court case, Carolyn. It's a picnic. Loosen up."

Was that the problem? She'd been too stiff? Too formal with Bobby? But she knew no other way. Had no experience with anything but court. There, she excelled. Here…

She couldn't be more out of her element if she'd been swimming with sharks.

"Here," Nick said, thrusting a potato sack at her. "You and Angela take this one, and I'll go make friends with Bobby. And us boys will challenge you girls."

Angela laughed, the sound tinkling in the summer air like coins dropping into a jar. "Oh, the girls will win. Girls always win."

"Want to bet a piece of pie on that?" Nick said.

"Sure!" Angela turned to Carolyn. "We can beat 'em, can't we, Carolyn? Oh, I mean, Miss Duff." Her little face sobered, the mirth wiped away with those two last words.

Carolyn had never felt more like a party pooper in her life.

"Sure we can, Angela," Carolyn said, holding out the sack so that they each could step inside. "And…call me Carolyn."

CHAPTER FIVE

NICK reached the finish line, breathless and in a pig pile of arms, legs and laughing small children and uncomfortable lawyers. He bent over, helped Bobby to his feet. "Not bad for a couple of amateurs, huh?"

The little boy beamed. "That was fun. I never did that before." Bobby's chest expanded with pride. "And we won. You must be really good at this."

"Nah, just lots of experience. My dad and my brother are the true reigning Lawford potato sack champs." Nick winked at Bobby.

"Your dad does this with you?" The boy's face fell six inches, and something clutched at Nick's heart.

"Well, he did, but now he's too old. And frankly," Nick said, pressing a hand to the ache in his back, "I think I might be, too." That struck him—that he was getting past the age where he should be doing this kind of thing, and yet it didn't bother him as much as he'd expected it would.

He'd had fun with Bobby, and for a second it felt like Bobby was his nephew. A cousin. Maybe even his own kid.

Now *that* was a weird sensation. Never before had Nick imagined having kids of his own. That had been one of those thoughts a million miles off in the future, like retirement planning. He shook it off. He wasn't the kind to raise a family. He'd tried marriage once, screwed it up and had no intentions of going there again.

Bobby and Nick started to walk toward the grandstand, where Mary was holding a trio of trophies for first, second and third place. Across the line of sack racers, Nick caught sight of Carolyn and Angela. He chuckled. Poor Carolyn. She looked about as comfortable out here as a porcupine at a balloon factory. She was back to being the stiff, straitlaced Bostonian he remembered from college. Getting her to loosen up had been half the fun of dating her. But apparently, Carolyn had gone right back to who she used to be—and that rigid persona didn't mix well with kids.

"It must be nice," Bobby said.

"Must be nice, what?" Nick asked, drawing his attention back to the boy.

"To have a dad who shows you how to race like a sack of potatoes."

Nick's gaze strayed to Carolyn again, and he

could have smacked himself upside the head. Of course. Everything about the day made sense. Her discomfort around the children. Her difficulty connecting. Her reluctance to join in on the crafts, the games.

It wasn't just that she'd lived in Boston. Or that she wasn't used to being around kids. Carolyn had much, much more going on than that.

Nick may be clueless when it came to what little girls might like for toys, but he had at least grown up in a two-parent family. Two parents who were still alive, still sitting at either end of the Thanksgiving table.

He hadn't watched his father get gunned down buying a gallon of milk. Then been sent to live with a woman who'd hated his existence.

He hadn't forgotten that hole in Carolyn's past, but he hadn't quite realized the impact of it on her, not until today. How hard it must be for her to be around children who'd experienced similar tragedies, to listen to other kids and parents who were working hard to maintain their families against tough odds. And then to see all these kids who were lost souls in foster families, being brought up by strangers?

Regret ran through Nick with a stab. How could he have been so cavalier as to suggest Carolyn was being formal? Lawyerish? Damn, he was a moron. Later, he vowed, he would apologize. Find a way to make it up to her. And most of all, help her make the whole day run much easier.

"Oh, look, Nick. Ours is gold. Do you think it's real?" Bobby was asking.

Nick followed where Bobby was pointing at the six-inch trophy, simply a gold-embellished pillar. He doubted it was anything more than real aluminum, and that the sheen came from gold spray paint. But he'd been a kid, too, and knew what it meant to a boy of that age to believe in the impossible.

He bent down to Bobby and smiled. "Absolutely. It looks real to me."

"I wish my mom could see it." Bobby sighed. He squinted against the bright sun as he looked up at Nick. "She was too sick to come today. So she stayed home. Lots of days she's too sick. But maybe when I bring this home, she'll feel better?"

Another slam into Nick's chest, that brought him up short. Drew him a thousand miles away from this being just fun and games and into something so much more. Something that could—

Have an impact on this kid's life.

An awesome sense of responsibility weighed on Nick's shoulders, a weight he'd never felt before. He tried it on, sure at first that being so used to not reporting to anyone, not being in charge of anyone but himself, that he'd resist the feeling of being needed by anyone.

But…

He looked at Bobby, at the kid's wide eyes, waiting for an answer, for someone to reassure him that his world would be okay, and decided he could do this. For this one day.

"I'm sure she will," Nick said. He might not be able to make up for Bobby's ill mother, for the boy not having a father—or for the potato sack races that Carolyn and all the girls like her had missed—but he could make one boy's day shine. Shine as bright as that trophy.

If there was one thing Nick was good at, it was showing somebody how to have fun. And maybe, in doing that with Bobby, he'd find a way to fill that weird hole in his own life, too.

Last place.

Carolyn had never come in last in anything in her entire life. From the sullen looks Angela kept sending her way, her partner in the potato sack race never had, either. "That was fun, wasn't it?"

"Where's Nick?" Angela said in response. Apparently that was a no.

"He's on the stage. He and Bobby came in… first."

"*And* they got a trophy." Angela shot her an accusatory glare.

"You still get a ribbon for participating," Carolyn said, trying to keep an upbeat tone. "And there are other games. Lots of chances to win yet."

"Here comes Nick!" Angela broke away from Carolyn and dashed toward her knight in shining armor.

Mary wove her way through the crowd and up to Carolyn. "How's it going so far?"

Carolyn groaned. "I'm getting my tubes tied."

"That bad, huh?"

"I am so not cut out for mothering. I don't think I could be trusted with a puppy at this point. In fact, don't even send me home with a houseplant. I'd kill the thing with boredom."

"Oh, it can't be that bad."

Carolyn gestured toward Nick, who had Bobby mounted on his shoulders, and Angela trotting alongside. Two people, apparently Angela's foster parents, had joined them. Angela was proudly making introductions. "See the Pied Piper of children. Note the lonely old maid who drove them away."

Mary laughed. "Maybe you should join forces with Nick. After all, the whole point of today is to engage the kids. And if it all works out, you can take it a step further."

"A step further?"

"And sign up for the Be-a-Buddy program." Mary made a sweeping gesture, indicating the crowd of children and adults. "That's what this is all about. A trial run of sorts. If the day is successful, we're hoping to get a lot of the sponsors to be a part of the buddy program and continue interacting with these kids. So many of them really need a strong role model in their lives. Someone who can see them on a regular basis and do enriching, fun activities."

Enriching? Fun? Strong role model? With *kids*? Mary had her confused with someone else.

Carolyn put up her hands. "I am the last person who should be involved in that. You know my schedule, Mary. You know what my life is like."

"I do," Mary said gently. "And that's exactly why I think you should be a part of this. I think you need it more than the kids do." She gave Carolyn's arm a squeeze, then walked away.

It should have been easy to walk away.

The picnic had broken up. The children had begun boarding the buses or getting into cars to go home, loaded up with toys and cookies, their faces filled with delight—and disappointment that the day was over. Nick had earned a tight hug goodbye and an explosion of gratitude from both Angela and Bobby, then noticed the little boy gave Carolyn a stiff handshake.

He could read the longing in her eyes, though, the moment of hesitation when he'd thought she might reach out and pull the boy into a hug. Then Carolyn had drawn back into herself, the moment of softness gone. She'd become the bulldog again.

The woman he'd known so briefly back in law school disappeared as quickly as a feather in the wind. Disappointment slammed him in the chest. He'd hoped maybe Carolyn could have loosened up, had a good time, but then again, he hadn't exactly helped a whole lot in that area, had he?

He'd had good intentions and gotten distracted by activities with the other kids. Leaving Carolyn to fend for herself. He'd let her down again, even though he hadn't meant to.

"Oh, look, she came."

Nick turned to find Mary, the event's organizer, who had come up beside him. For a second he expected Mary to be talking about Carolyn, then realized that wouldn't make any sense. He really needed to clear his head. Every other thought was about Carolyn Duff, for Pete's sake. "She who?"

"Bobby's mother. Bobby said she hadn't been feeling well this morning, and I didn't think she'd make it to the picnic. He was so disappointed."

But she's here. She knew how much this mattered to Bobby, so she came." Mary smiled. "She's one tough lady."

Bobby darted across the field toward the woman, just as Carolyn wandered over and joined Nick and Mary. She shaded her eyes against the sun. "Is that Bobby's mother?"

"Yep. Oh, look, he's waving at us," Mary said. "I think he wants to introduce you to her."

"Oh, I don't think—" Carolyn began.

"I think you should," Mary interrupted. "It'll only take a second."

Nick could see Carolyn's hesitation, sensed it in the set of her shoulders, the tension in her jaw. He remembered what she had told him about her childhood, about the years she had spent with her cold, unforgiving aunt Greta. Alone in a big, empty Victorian house, with no other real family. Carolyn, Nick knew, would feel uncomfortable in a family situation. Even though she'd said earlier that she'd wished she'd met his family, when they'd been together, she'd always found an excuse not to meet his parents, his siblings. The very idea had seemed to scare her.

The bulldog of Lawford could take on criminals, put them behind bars for years, but when it came to barbecues and holidays, she backed down and turned tail.

"Come on, it won't be so bad," Nick said, slipping his hand into hers. To offer support…friendship. Nothing more. But her delicate fingers were cool against his broad palm, the feel of her as familiar as a sunrise.

She looked up at him, defiant and brave. "I never said it would be. Let's go." Despite her words, Carolyn didn't let go of Nick's hand until they were across the field.

There they met up with Bobby and a small, thin brunette woman who looked tired but happy. Bobby stood before her, one arm holding on to hers, the other clutching his trophy. Pride shone in every inch of his face. "Nick, Miss Duff, I want you to meet my momma."

"I heard wonderful things about you both." The woman smiled. When she did, ten years were wiped off her face, and the difficulties of her life, so clear in her face, in the threadbare floral shirt and worn jeans she wore, seemed to be erased. "I'm Pauline Lester." She extended a hand. The trio shook and exchanged introductions.

"They bought me toys, Momma," Bobby said. "So many, I don't think I can fit them in my room. Do I have to give them back?"

His mother laughed. "No, you can keep them all, sweetheart." She drew her son against her, his wiry body cradling gently into her thin frame, her arm a shield and comfort. Then she met Nick and Carolyn's gaze. Tears of gratitude welled in her eyes, but didn't spill over. "Thank you. I can't even begin to tell you how much this means to my son, to me."

"It was nothing," Carolyn said, wishing now that she had spent even more on Bobby, that she could afford to buy this mother and her son a whole house, furnish it from top to bottom. Pull an entire extreme makeover for this struggling family. "We just tried to get him something he'd like."

"Oh, you did, and then some. Bobby's a wonderful boy." She ruffled his head. "He doesn't need much."

"Just you, Momma," he said, burying his face in her shirt, as if inhaling her perfume. Imprinting her memory.

Carolyn's throat swelled shut. Why had Mary paired her with this boy? The one who brought up everything from her own childhood? The parents she had lost—one she'd never known, the other that had been stolen from her. Her heart broke for Bobby—because she'd been where he was, wanting so hard to hold on to someone who wasn't guaranteed to stay.

She felt a touch against her and looked down. Nick had slipped his hand into hers again. He gave her palm a squeeze.

Whoa, there was a surprise. He'd been paying attention and he not only knew, he understood. And was telling her he was there. Twice now he had done this. Gratitude flooded her and she sent him a smile.

"Did you see my trophy, Momma? I think it might be real gold." Bobby hoisted up his first place trophy, beaming with pride. "Nick and I won the potato sack race. He said he and his dad were the potato winners all the time."

"Is that so? Well, you picked a good partner, then."

"And Nick said that I'm his buddy." Bobby's smiled widened. "I never had a buddy like that before."

"That's wonderful, Bobby." His mother drew in a breath, then let it out in a shudder. She coughed, and Carolyn could see exhaustion claiming her. "Let's go home now."

"Are you okay, Momma?"

She patted his shoulder. "Just fine, Bobby. Just fine."

But all the adults could hear the lie the mother told her son.

"Thank you again," Pauline told Nick and Carolyn. "It's really nice to see Bobby smiling again."

Then she turned and left, with her son at her side, his hand on her arm, protective and doting.

A family, no matter how small, but a family all the same. In a two-person cocoon.

"What is it with you two?"

After Bobby and Pauline Lester had left, Nick hung around to help finish cleaning up. He was just about to leave when he turned to find Mary Hudson, the event's organizer, standing beside him. She had her arms crossed over her chest, and though there were faint shadows of exhaustion beneath her eyes from the long day, he could see the sharp look of inquisitiveness in her hazel gaze. "Us two who?" he asked.

"Oh, please. Like you don't know. You and Carolyn. Everyone within a three-county area can tell there's unfinished business between the two of you." She picked up a stray piece of trash on the ground and tossed it into a nearby barrel. "And I know, because I work with Carolyn every day. She refuses to talk about you. Whenever Carolyn is silent, that's a sure sign she's hiding something big."

Carolyn wouldn't talk about him with other people. Nick didn't know whether to take that as a compliment or an insult. "It's all in the past."

"Not that far in the past, from what I can see."

"Carolyn has moved on, I'm sure." Nick was probing and he knew it. Shamelessly probing.

"No, she hasn't. She spends every minute of

her day working. Stuck in that office, poring over her computer, or in court. She has no love life, no life at all, really. She needs a man."

And from the way Mary was eyeing him, giving him a visual résumé read, he'd apparently already been interviewed and hired for the job. But Mary didn't know the history between Carolyn and him. There were some roads that couldn't—and definitely shouldn't—be traveled twice.

"I'm sure she'll meet someone," Nick said, then turned away, tearing his gaze away from Carolyn, even as doing so seemed to tear something in his gut.

But it was better this way. He knew it, knew it so well he should have written the words on the walls of his house. They were already scrawled all over his heart. He'd screwed up when he'd married Carolyn, rushing into a marriage he'd had no business proposing, because he was after the chase more than the big picture.

Even now, he didn't have the desire to settle down fully. Really become a fully functioning grown-up who mowed the lawn on Saturdays, changed diapers on a regular basis and paid into a college fund. Until then, he should steer clear of women, especially women like Carolyn, who made getting serious into an art form.

"Nick, wait."

He pivoted back.

"I promise, no more talk about your love life," Mary said, holding up her hands in surrender. "This is about the kids. You did such a great job today."

"Thanks."

"You're going to make a great dad someday."

"I'm leaving that job to my sisters and brother. Plenty of Gilberts to go around already. I'm better in the indulgent uncle role."

"Too bad," Mary said. "Because I saw true parenting genius. You brought Angela out of her shell, got her talking her head off all day. Bobby had fun. It was incredible."

Nick didn't reply. If he was such great parent material, he'd have been married and had kids of his own by now. But he'd totally messed up his one attempt at marriage, and he wasn't about to go running down that heartbreak hill, not again. "I should get going. Thanks for a great day. You pulled off a hell of an event."

"Don't go, not yet. Would you mind talking with Jean Klein? She works for the Lawford Department of Child Services. She and I were wondering if you could do us a favor," Mary said. "Well, not us so much, but Bobby."

"Bobby? Sure, just tell me what you need."

"It's easier if Jean explains." Mary led him over to one of the picnic tables, where Carolyn was already sitting and chatting with another woman, whom Mary introduced as Jean. Nick slipped into a seat opposite the two women. Mary sat down beside him.

"First," Jean began, "I wanted to say I appreciate your time and the time of all the other attorneys today. It was wonderful to see the kids so happy, but especially Bobby. He had a great time, engaging with other people. He hasn't been adapting so well to the challenges of the last few months. It's been really hard on him since his father died."

"His father died?" Nick asked. He glanced at Carolyn, and saw a deep well of sympathy in her eyes.

Oh, damn. Of all people, Carolyn was the last person who should be sitting here, hearing this. Not after all she'd gone through as a kid. It had to be bringing up some awful memories. The sudden urge to shield her rushed over him. But she was an adult, and had made it clear that she didn't need him—or anyone else. So he sat where he was and returned his attention to the conversation.

Jean nodded. "It was tragic. A drive-by shooting last year."

Poor Bobby. What an awful thing for a little boy to have to go through. The urge to reach out to Carolyn again doubled. His hand snuck across the divide between them on the bench, there if she needed it, or not if she didn't.

"To compound the boy's difficulties," Jean went on, "his mother has been in and out of the hospital."

"He mentioned she's sick."

"Breast cancer. Though the worst seems to be behind her now, or we hope so. I think part of what's making it so hard for her to win this battle is worrying about her son. Money was tight before Bobby's father died, but afterward, there wasn't any insurance, and with his mother sick, they've been living paycheck to paycheck in this tiny little apartment you can barely call a home. And when his mother gets sick, he sometimes doesn't have anyplace to go."

Jean drew in a breath, let it go. Her concern for the child was clear in her voice, her mannerisms. Nick's respect for the case worker multiplied. He could only imagine how hard it must be for her to deal with this kind of thing every day, when all he worked with was business law. None of this heavy, emotional baggage.

"All the other times, Bobby's grandmother was able to take care of Bobby, but now his grandmother is simply too old and recently had to be moved to a nursing home. The last time Bobby's mother was hospitalized, we had no choice but to send him to foster care."

"Foster care?" Carolyn repeated. "Living with strangers?"

Nick's gaze slid again to Carolyn. He could see she understood far too well what that must have been like for Bobby. He read it in her face, in the concern in her voice. Although he knew, from what she'd told him, that life with her aunt Greta had been awful, he began to realize, just in what was etched in her eyes, how much he hadn't known about his whirlwind wife, how much of her past he'd missed, in the rush to the altar. He hadn't been paying attention then—but he was now.

"I'm sure Bobby didn't do well there," Carolyn said.

Jean shook her head. "Too many changes, too quick. It's been incredibly difficult for him. He wants his family back, and well, that's not going to happen. It's hard for a child that age to understand that the world is never going to go back to the way it used to be."

Nick swallowed hard. "Yeah. I understand."

Carolyn was mute. But Nick could read, in the set of her shoulders, that she empathized with Bobby, probably more than anyone at this table. His hand snaked closer, inching across the rough pine surface, but still he was too far away from her, and she had drawn into herself, her body stiff, everything about her saying she was a sole sentry in her feelings.

"That's why I was so amazed to see him smiling

today," Jean continued. "When I say I haven't seen that boy smile in months, I mean it."

"I had no idea," Nick said. "So many of these children today have such difficult lives and yet they were happy, as if nothing had happened."

This was a world Nick had never seen. It had always existed; he'd just been going along blithely with his life, never really seeing how others lived right alongside him. But now, to have it presented in person, with big brown eyes, made him sit up and take notice.

"They're resilient," Jean said. "And determined. The kids are the ones that make my job rewarding."

"Hey, Mary, can I get a hand over here?" One of the volunteers shouted, her arms overloaded with leftovers from the food table.

Mary rose. "Sorry, I have to go clean up."

"I'll help," Carolyn said. The two of them headed off to catch a teetering pile of bowls just before it came tumbling down. Nick suspected Carolyn had left the table, not so much to help, but because the subject matter was hitting a little too close to home.

He watched her for a minute and saw her slip back into being efficient, strong Carolyn. The woman who betrayed no emotion. Nick brought his hands together in a tight knot and let out a sigh.

Carolyn and her walls. If only she hadn't had

so many of them, maybe there would have been hope for them. For their marriage to survive.

Hell, who was he kidding? He hadn't tried so hard to scale those walls. Doing so would have meant buckling down, getting serious. Being the kind of man who really worked hard at his marriage. He'd gotten married on a lark. Then, when faced with the reality of what he'd done, taken the easy way out. Even now, three years later, Nick didn't feel any more ready or prepared to make that leap than he had before.

"Anyway," Jean said, interrupting Nick's thoughts, "back to the reason I wanted to talk to you. I noticed that Bobby seemed to latch on to you. He opened up. Had fun." Jean smiled. "That's also something Bobby hasn't done in months. We were hoping that for this weekend, maybe you would consider being his buddy."

"Buddy?"

"It's part of the Be-a-Buddy program," Jean explained. "Sort of like the Big Sisters/Big Brothers program." Nick nodded his understanding. "You'd hang out with Bobby, like you did today, and take him places. Have fun. Let him be a kid. His mother's not feeling well and having a rough time of it lately, so this could be the break she needs for a few days. Plus, Bobby needs a strong male role model. And, most of all, he needs to laugh."

Nick shifted on the hard wooden picnic seat. He splayed his hands across the table. Strong male role model? Him? Ha, if only they knew him. He wasn't anyone's role model, more a model of how to be a cut-up in the classroom. "Jean, I'd like to help, but—"

"Don't say no. He needs you." Jean laid a palm atop his. "Mary told me you've undergone a criminal background check because you're involved with a youth basketball program at the YMCA. That clears one hurdle for us already, and allows you to get started with Bobby immediately. And if it's too much for you to do alone, feel free to ask a friend or family member to help you out. Sometimes that makes it easier to make that bridge with a child."

Unbidden, Nick's gaze sought out the one other person left on the picnic grounds who would understand Bobby Lester. Someone else who had lost a father…had her childhood ripped away. And someone who could…

Maybe be the ying to his yang. He'd always been the clown, where she'd always been the serious one. Maybe together…?

He watched Carolyn finish the clean-up of the food table, her movements stiff and severe. What had happened to the Carolyn he had met so many years ago? The woman he had managed to get to loosen up, to laugh, and then finally fallen in love with? The woman who had, for one brief moment in time, made him consider growing up, maybe take life a little more seriously?

Could he—if he helped her find her way back to those days—find where he had lost that thread in their marriage? Make up for the way he had messed things up? And maybe if he repaired that damage, ensure a better future down the road, for both of them?

He thought of Bobby. Of the laughter that had bubbled out of that boy today but had not entirely covered the deep dark sadness that lingered behind his eyes.

Nick might be the one who could provide the fun and games, but to truly touch Bobby's life, he knew only one other person in the world who would understand that world. Who could reach into the gloomy spaces in that boy's heart and really draw him out.

"I'll do it," he said. "But on one condition."

CHAPTER SIX

"No way."

Carolyn stood in her office on Sunday morning, hands on her hips, refusing Mary for the four hundredth time. "Absolutely not."

"One holiday weekend, Carolyn. Not a lifetime commitment. Think of it as a vacation."

Carolyn turned away and sank into her leather chair. "With Nick? That's not a vacation, Mary. That's like one big—"

"Ball of temptation. I've seen him up close, Carolyn, and he is a hottie, in all capital letters."

Carolyn shook her head. "And you are an incurable romantic. Seeing happy endings where there aren't any. I have work to do. Tell Nick to find someone else. Surely the man has friends. And I know he has family."

"He wants you." Mary arched a brow and grinned. "Wants *you*," she stressed again.

"I don't want him."

Liar, liar. Everything within Carolyn had wanted Nick yesterday. It had taken a supreme act of willpower not to give in to the desire to touch him. To feel the warmth of the sun on his arms. To curve against his chest, just as she had years before. Because her body didn't forget. Her mind remembered every inch of that man's body. Even if the rest of her knew better.

Knew getting involved with him, especially a second time, was a bad idea.

"Either way, you're too late," Mary said. "Because—" she paused a beat, long enough for Carolyn to hear the familiar ding of the elevator "—he's here now."

"He's *here?* How could you do that? I told you—"

"Overruled, Counselor." Mary grinned, then headed out of Carolyn's office, leaving the door ajar.

Before she could react, Nick entered her office, and Carolyn's breath left her. For a long second she didn't see Bobby, didn't see Mary pass by, wave and head downstairs, didn't see anything but the vibrant blue of Nick's eyes and the familiar curve of his grin.

He was here. Just when she'd thought he was out of her life again for good. And damn if her heart didn't react as predictably as a moth to a bug light.

"Nick. I'm sorry. I just found out about—"

"Miss Duff...uh, Carolyn," Bobby cut in. "Nick told me we're going to the fair today. You're coming, right? Nick said you're really good at the games and he said you can win a prize for me."

The boy's eyes were wide, his smile full of hope. And Carolyn was caught in Nick's already woven web. She shot him a glare. She thought of everything Jean had told them yesterday, and guilt rocketed through her. Bobby was relying on them, counting on Nick and her to provide a few of the good times his life had been so devoid of lately. There was no way out of this.

Still, she stalled. "A little pre-event disclosure would have been nice, Mr. Gilbert."

"I didn't want you to ready an objection, Miss Duff."

"My docket is already full," she said, indicating the pile of work on her desk. "I don't have room in my agenda for extraneous field trips."

Bobby looked from one adult to the other, completely confused.

"Counselor, I think you need a recess. It is Sunday, after all, and the courts are closed."

Carolyn ran a hand over her face. Nick was not making this easy. Why wouldn't he listen? Didn't he understand? What if something went wrong? What if something happened? Didn't he read the statistics about holiday weekends? The drunk drivers, the partyers starting fights, the fireworks accidents, the looters taking advantage of closed stores—

The nightmares ran through Carolyn's mind at double time. "Nick, I don't think you're taking into account all the criminal element variables."

"It's a simple field trip, Carolyn. Not a foray into the depths of Sing-Sing."

Her heart began to race, her lungs pumping faster. She rocketed back two dozen years, unable to stop the comparisons to her own life. What if?

What if something went wrong? What if she couldn't stop it? What if Bobby got hurt?

Bobby stood there, wearing a short white T-shirt decorated with a flag, and little navy shorts. His hair was freshly combed, his old, nearly worn-through sneakers neatly tied. Trusting. Innocent. Again, she thought, what if?

"Nick, I really can't," Carolyn said.

Bobby's face fell.

"Counselor, I request a sidebar. On behalf of my client." Nick gestured toward Bobby.

Carolyn knew she wasn't going to be able to get rid of Nick easily. That persistence had been what had worn her down all those years ago in college. She refused to let him win again this time, though. She laid her pen on her desk. "Bobby, would you like to sit at the desk outside my office? It's

Mary's desk and she has candy in the dish. You can have two pieces."

A grin spread from one ear to the other, then halted. Bobby looked up at Nick, as if he was afraid someone would tell him no. Nick gave Bobby a nod, then bent down to whisper in his ear. "Go ahead. And if you take three, I won't tell anyone. By the way, I bet that chair spins pretty fast."

Bobby hurried through the open door and climbed onto Mary's leather chair. A second later he was swiveling in a circle and sucking on a peppermint.

"Nick, I don't have time for this. I have a plea bargain to work on, a bunch of depositions to review…" She waved a vague hand at her desk. Excuses, she knew, but valid ones. "You'll do just fine with Bobby on your own."

"We both know it's not about your workload, Carolyn. What's the real problem?" He leaned closer. "Don't you want to spend time with me? And Bobby?"

She let out a gust. "Not everything in my life revolves around you."

"Then what is it?"

"Don't you read the paper? Aren't you worried something might go wrong?"

"Something…" He stared at her. "What could possibly go wrong?" His old devil-may-care smile curved up his lips. "What, some rogue carousel horse might run amok?"

Carolyn paced her office, frustration pushing her steps. "I'm not treating this as a joke, Nick. A thousand things could happen."

He got in front of her, preventing her from wearing any further path in the carpet. "You can't live your life around the possibility of what might happen. You have to take risks."

"With someone else's child? What if—"

"And what if everything goes just fine? What if we all have a good time? What would be so wrong with that?"

She shook her head. Nick didn't understand. He hadn't lived through what she had. He hadn't had a childhood where he woke up in the middle of the night, screaming from nightmares. She knew the dangers, understood what could lurk in the world. "You don't need me to go."

"That's where you're wrong. Bobby *does* need you. You specifically."

"Me? Why? He's barely said three words to me since we met."

"You know why," Nick said quietly. His gaze met hers, and a beat passed between them. "Because Bobby's father was murdered, just like yours. You are the only one, Carolyn, the only one who can truly understand what it's like for him."

The words slammed into Carolyn, words that she thought would have no effect on her, not anymore. She'd been over that for so long, but now she glanced out the door, at the little boy spinning in the chair a few feet away, his head downcast, his shoulders hunched with a weight that only a few, a select group that Carolyn was part of, none of them by choice, could recognize. Her eyes blurred and then she no longer saw Bobby.

She saw herself.

Her mind rocketed back to that day—that day in the convenience store, when she'd cowered, sobbing, by the milk, thinking if she could make herself really, really small, maybe the bad man wouldn't notice her and he'd just go away. He'd leave, leave her and her father alone. He'd stop yelling, stop asking for money no one had.

But he hadn't stopped. And when her father had tried to stand up to him, tried to make him go away, because he'd been scaring Carolyn—*telling her to shut up, shut the hell up*—his gun in her face, and then her father was there, and the gun had gone off, the explosion so loud Carolyn thought she'd never hear again.

And her father falling, falling, falling, so slow, she had run forward, trying to catch him, thinking if she could catch him, she could stop it all. But she hadn't been able to stop him from falling. Stop the blood. Stop his life from leaking onto the tile floor, into a sticky, copper-smelling puddle beside her. Even when the policemen had come and taken away the bad man, and then her father, Carolyn hadn't wanted to believe it was over. Hadn't wanted to leave. She'd just stared at that crimson spot on the floor, willing it to go away, for all of it to disappear.

She sucked in a breath, tried to steady herself again, clutching her desk, the scent of copper so strong again in her nose she thought she might be sick. But no, it was over. It was over. Breathe. Breathe.

She had been nine. Bobby had been four. Was there ever a good age to hear that someone had stolen your father?

"He needs you, Carolyn," Nick repeated.

She shook her head and spun away from Nick, away from the sight of Bobby, the memories his presence evoked, to face the window, her gaze going to the sunny view of Lawford below her. The city was quiet, the downtown area empty as a cemetery. "Not me, Nick. Please, not me."

Nick came up behind her, his hands going to her shoulders, a light touch, but so heavy inside her. "I think you need him, too. Mary says you work all the time. You have no life. This might be exactly the right thing for you."

She wheeled around, out of his grasp. "How do you know what I need?" she whispered, keeping her voice low, so Bobby didn't overhear. "We were only married four days, Nick. Knew each other for, what, three weeks? You think you really got to know me in that time? You didn't. Not really. Let's not kid ourselves."

"No, I guess I didn't." A shadow dropped over his face and he took a step back. Then it was gone, and he cleared his throat. "This isn't about us anyway. This is about him. It's one weekend. A fair, some fireworks. Let's put our differences aside for two days, for Bobby's sake. And maybe, just maybe, we can make a difference in his life." Nick's gaze met hers. "You used to tell me how awful it was living with your aunt Greta. How cold she was. How would things have been different for you when you were a kid, if someone had stepped in and played mom and dad—or simply played fairy godparents like we would be—for you, just for a weekend?"

Aunt Greta. She'd tried to forget the icy aunt who had raised her after Carolyn's father's death, a woman so devoid of emotion she might as well have been a stone.

Tears sprang to Carolyn's eyes, and a lump wedged so thick in her throat, she didn't think she'd ever get it dislodged. She shook her head, her fists clenched together. "That's not playing fair, Nick."

"I'm not playing anything, Carolyn." He reached up and cupped her jaw, his touch tender and gentle. "I've made my case, Counselor. While I await your verdict, I'm going to go join the rest of the jury in the outer office before he turns into the Tasmanian devil on a serious sugar high."

Nick told himself not to be disappointed. That Carolyn had every right to say no. He'd sprung the idea on her at the last minute, when she'd had a stack of work on her desk and—

And damn it, he could give a thousand reasons why she might be justified in saying no, but that didn't mean he liked a single one of them.

"How's come Miss Duff didn't want to go?"

"She had a lot of work to do," Nick said. He and Bobby wandered the noisy, brightly lit midway of the Lawford Fourth of July Weekend Festival, a stack of tickets for rides in one hand and the remains of a sticky cotton candy poof in the other. Little blue sugar crystals coated Bobby's lips and dotted his T-shirt, but he had a smile on his face and a belly that looked full enough to burst.

"Can we ride the Roaring Dragon ride next?" he asked, taking the cotton candy from Nick and devouring the rest. "Dragons are my favorite thing in the world."

"Why don't we let that candy settle first? I don't think we want your snack to make a reappearance." He might not know a lot about kids, but he did know enough to know mixing sugar and fast movement too soon would be a disaster.

"Okay." Bobby tossed the empty cotton candy stick into the trash then stopped in front of one of the carney stands. Stuffed animals in a range of size marched across the front of the stand, swinging tantalizingly in the light breeze.

"Come on up, take your chances!" A skinny man, dressed in jeans and a bright-red T-shirt advertising the fair sat on the edge of the booth, leaning out, waving at all who passed. "Throw the balls into the basket, win a prize. Get in all three, win your choice."

"Can we do it, Nick?" Bobby tugged on his sleeve, practically jumping up and down. "Can we? I really want that stuffed dragon. *Dragon Tales* is like my favorite show ever. And I really love dragons. Only not the kind that breathe fire. Fire is kind of scary, but dragons are cool."

Nick chuckled. How could he resist that? Earlier this morning, Bobby had been morose, worried about his mother, who had been so sick, Jean said, that she'd still been in bed when Jean had picked Bobby up and brought him to meet Nick at Carolyn's office. That had had Nick worried. He was good when a kid was bubbly. Full of energy. Ready to play. But dealing with an emotional, moody child—

Not his best suit. Which was why he'd called on Carolyn. She was the one he'd hoped could handle the tough stuff. Thankfully, once he and Bobby had reached the fair, the somber mood had lifted, and now Bobby seemed to have left all his troubles behind. He and Nick had had a blast so far, riding tons of rides, stopping in at some of the exhibits and wandering through the petting zoo. If it meant keeping Bobby in the good humor Nick was comfortable with, Nick would play any game at the fair.

"Think you can win it, Nick?" Bobby asked again.

"Sure, I can try. But I have to warn you, this one is not my area of expertise."

"No, it's not. It's mine."

Nick turned, sure he'd imagined the voice. But no, there she stood, a smile on her face, wearing shorts and a T-shirt, her blond hair back in a ponytail, looking so much like the Carolyn he used to know back in college that he couldn't believe she was the same woman he'd seen in the office a couple hours earlier. It was as if stepping outside the doors of the county prosecutor's office had made her shed the skin of the strict, tough Carolyn and brought her back to the woman he had fallen in love with all those years ago.

"Miss Duff!" Bobby exclaimed. "You came."

"Call me Carolyn," she reminded gently, then bent down to his level. "And yes, I came, because Nick here is no good at winning these games and I couldn't let you go home empty-handed."

She glanced up at Nick and their eyes met, held. For one long heartbeat, Nick knew. She was here for more than giving this boy a stuffed animal. It was about giving him the experience he was missing because he'd lost that half of his family so critical to normalcy.

Because despite all her worries about safety, just like Nick had thought, she understood what Bobby was going through, and didn't want him to miss out on what she had in her childhood. For once, Nick had read Carolyn right, and he wondered whether if he had done it once, he could do it again.

"So," Carolyn said, rising and brushing her hands together, "shall we do this?"

Bobby nodded. "Can you get the dragon?"

"Anything you want, Bobby."

Nick slapped down a five-dollar bill and the man placed three balls before Carolyn. He explained the game, then stood to the side and demonstrated with one swift throw how easy it was to land a wiffle ball in the wooden basket, the kind usually used for gathering fruit. "He makes it look easy," Nick whispered to Carolyn.

"They always do, but if it were easy, everyone would win and the fair wouldn't make any money." She bent down next to Bobby. "Okay, I'll share the secret with you on how to win, but you have to keep it a secret. My father told it to me and now I'll tell it to you."

Bobby's eyes widened with excitement at being let in on a secret. He nodded solemnly. "Okay."

Keeping her voice low, Carolyn demonstrated with the ball in her hand. "You need to get as close as you're allowed to, according to the rules. You want to toss underhanded, put a little spin on it and don't throw too hard. The basket isn't very deep and your goal is to aim for the lip of the basket, where the sweet spot is."

"What's a sweet spot?"

Carolyn smiled. "The best spot to hit, so that the ball will drop right into the basket." She rose, juggling one of the balls in her right hand. "Watch."

Nick watched, amazed, as Carolyn stepped up to the booth, leaned forward, but not so much that she extended over the counter, and tossed the ball. The white sphere rose upward in an arc, spinning as it arched toward the basket, pinging off the rim, then dropped lightly into the basket and settled in the bottom.

"You did it!" Bobby jumped up beside her. "You did it!"

Several people who had stopped by the booth to watch Carolyn shoot applauded her success. Nick, however, wasn't impressed so much with her aim as he was with the change that had come over Carolyn when she'd leaned down and talked to Bobby. Her entire demeanor had relaxed, and she had become someone else. Someone who reached out, extended a thread, then knotted that connection into a rope.

It was an entirely new side of her. A side he realized he liked. Very much.

"Do it again," Bobby said. "All three gets to pick any toy."

Carolyn shot Nick a smile. "Nothing like a little pressure."

"You can do it," he said, taking a step closer.

Carolyn wavered for a moment. Nick's breath, warm against her neck, sent a wave of desire rushing through her. She forgot all about the carnival game. The fairgoers. Why she was there. All she wanted to do was lean into Nick's touch and see where that particular game of chance got her.

Then Bobby tugged at her sleeve and brought her back to reality. "Can you do it again?"

"Sure, sure." Carolyn shot the second ball, then the third, sinking both of them into the basket. Around them, the crowd erupted into applause, the bell was rung announcing a winner, and Bobby sported the largest smile a child could. He chose a bright-green-and-red stuffed dragon that was nearly half his size and thanked Carolyn several times as they walked away.

"Wow! You are really good at that. Did your daddy win you a dragon, too?" Bobby clutched the dragon to his chest, as proud of the stuffed animal as a new parent.

"No, a bear. I still have it."

Bobby plucked at the dragon's scales, his fingers pulling at the yellow triangles, his gaze downcast. "Is your father still alive?"

"No, Bobby, he isn't," Carolyn said. She drew in a breath. This was harder to talk about than she expected—because she *never* talked about it. She'd put it behind her after that day, moved forward—charged forward, really, determined not to let one day become the moment that defined her life.

Yet, there had been moments when she'd been growing up when she had wished *someone* would have talked to her. Mentioned her father. Told her a story, told her it was okay to talk about what had happened. Aunt Greta had refused to mention the death of her brother, had buried the topic along with him at the cemetery. Leaving nine-year-old Carolyn to stuff those feelings inside, with nowhere to vent that volcano of fear, worry and hurt.

What Carolyn had needed most back then was a friend. A friend who understood. And as she looked down into Bobby's eyes, his fingers clutching that dragon as if the stuffed animal could ward off all the rest of the evil in the world, she knew he, too, needed a friend. "My father—" she swallowed "—he was killed by a bad man when I was nine."

Bobby bit his lip, clutched the dragon tighter. "A bad man hurt my daddy, too," he said, the words slow in coming. His teeth tugged at his lip some more, then he went on. "My daddy is in heaven now. And my mom, she has to go to the hospital a lot, sometimes for a long time. My grandma's too old to watch me, so when my mom is gone, I have to live with other people. Did you have to do that, too?"

Carolyn nodded, her voice lost in a swell of emotion. Oh, how she knew that life. Knew it too well. Poor Bobby. Carolyn's heart squeezed so tight she thought it might never beat properly again. Her throat closed, her breath caught, then she forced out a gust, extended a hand and—

Reached out. Tentative, she captured Bobby's free hand in her own. He hesitated, then the little palm warmed hers, fingers curling between her own, tightening into her grasp, holding on to her as firmly as he did the dragon. Now her heart swelled to bursting with compassion and she whispered a single wish to the heavens. That this boy would be safe forever, that the road ahead would be easy for Bobby Lester, because the one he was on had already been too hard. "I'm sorry, Bobby. I'm so sorry."

He looked up at her and nodded, understanding extending between them like a web. "Me, too."

Nick's arm stole around Carolyn's waist, strong, secure, *there*, and she let herself lean into his touch, needing him right then as much as Bobby needed her.

Then the three of them stopped and simply stood there, pretending they were watching the Ferris wheel make its slow spin. But really, not seeing anything at all but a blurry circle of lights.

CHAPTER SEVEN

JEAN met Nick and Carolyn, along with Bobby, outside the fair at nine that night, on the dot. She looked harried and overwhelmed, but grateful to see Bobby sporting a smiling face and arms full of prizes. "I take it you had a good time?"

Bobby nodded. "Uh-huh. It was really fun," he said. "Can we go every day?"

Jean laughed. "Sorry, Bobby, but the fair moves on to another town tomorrow."

The little boy swallowed, and accepted that information without complaint, disappointment clearly something he was used to. Nick's chest tightened. Once again Bobby's world and the one he'd grown up in were a thousand miles apart. He may not have been rich or spoiled, but he sure had been privileged, and indulged with happiness and family. Guilt rocketed through Nick, and in a weird way he wanted to give some of those years back, if only so that Bobby could have them instead.

Bobby shrugged, as if he didn't care, the bravado back in place. "That's all right. The fair was just okay anyway."

It wasn't okay, not by a long shot, not in Nick's book, but he was powerless to make the fair stay in town. To change the circumstances of one boy's life.

Carolyn met Nick's eye and he saw her bite back a sigh, just as he did, at the sound of Bobby's too-old speech. "Bobby won this mirror all by himself," Nick said, clapping the boy on the shoulder with the change of subject, hoping it would restore the child's good humor. Not really knowing what else to do. "He hit three balloons with the darts. He's got some seriously good aim. Probably see him in the Major Leagues someday."

That earned a smile. Hurrah.

"Good job, Bobby," Jean said.

"Thank you." Bobby, however, still didn't seem much happier. Nick looked to Carolyn for help.

"Tomorrow, Bobby, will be quite the adventurous evening. We'll be reconvening and attend the fireworks celebration."

Nick sent Carolyn a sidelong glance. *Reconvening? Celebration?* Bobby also gave her a baffled look. Carolyn just stood there, stiff as a board. What was wrong with her? It seemed like every time the boy got close to her, she put up this wall of formality.

She did it with Bobby; she did it with Nick. Here he'd thought they were making such great progress and that he could finally read her, understand what made her tick.

Obviously, he'd gotten it just as wrong this time as he had three years ago. Maybe she was right. Maybe he didn't understand her.

Or maybe he just needed to try harder.

"We'll have fun tomorrow, Bobby, I promise," Nick said, ruffling the boy's hair.

Bobby's smile spread so far across his face, Nick was sure it reached from one ear to the other. "You mean it? You're not just saying that? A lot of people make promises and then they have to break them. And…well, I'll understand if you can't come." He toed at the dirt beneath his worn sneakers, then looked up again. "I bet you're real busy."

Bobby stared at him, waiting for the answer. Nick knew what the boy was really asking. Would Nick be there—beyond this weekend. This fair. The fireworks tomorrow.

Would he be a real friend? And not just a guy making an empty promise?

Nick's gut tightened. He wasn't used to this. People expecting anything of him. Sure, there were expectations at work, but those ended when he walked out the door. In his personal life, he answered to no one, unless he counted

Bandit, and all the dog wanted was a can of food every morning, a walk every night and a reliable ball-throwing partner. Not exactly a major commitment.

Except for his whirlwind marriage to Carolyn, he had never really settled down with anything or anyone, and even then, four days wasn't any kind of commitment. Bobby was looking, Nick knew, for more. Not a lifetime, but more than Nick Gilbert had ever given before. He looked to Carolyn for a good answer, but she had already inserted that distance that she was so good at.

Why had Mary ever put the two of them in charge of children, specifically this one? Neither of them had what it took to connect, not over the long haul. Nick thought he could do this, but…

Damn, it was a lot harder than he'd thought.

"Sure," he managed finally, because what else could he say? When the boy looked at him like that, with such hope in his eyes, it made Nick want to run for president and change the world. "I'm your buddy, for as long as you want."

"Come on, Bobby," Jean said. "Time to go home." She took him by the hand, seeming to read the tension in the group. "Your mom is waiting and I'm sure she wants to hear all about your day. Plus, it's bedtime. You'll see Nick and Carolyn tomorrow for the fireworks."

Then Jean was gone, with Bobby in tow, leaving Nick and Carolyn alone.

"I should go, too," Carolyn said. But she didn't move. Her gaze caught his, and again he wondered if maybe one of the problems between them hadn't been that he hadn't read her right, but that he hadn't tried *hard enough* to read her.

He'd seen another side of her today, in the way she'd reached out to Bobby, let herself be vulnerable. A side he wanted to explore more. Letting her go now didn't seem like an option.

Nick turned and took Carolyn's hand, falling into touching her, relying on her, just as he always had before. His world had been rocked, and he sought the closest mountain he knew. "Stay," he said. "Please."

"I—" She cut off the sentence. "Okay. But let's get out of here. It's so busy. And noisy."

Nick nodded. "I know just the place." Still holding hands, he led her to his SUV, then held the door for her. She brushed by him as she moved to sit in the passenger's seat, giving him a hint of her perfume. Sweet floral notes, an undertone of jasmine. He leaned forward, unable to stop himself from getting close to her, and pressed his lips to her neck, inhaling the scent and leaving a long, lingering kiss along the delicate skin that curved beneath her blond tresses. Oh, so familiar.

So sweet. He was tempted to do more, to let his fingers walk along the same path, to take her in his arms, but he didn't. Carolyn paused, tense for one second, then she drew in a breath, let it out, along with his name. "Nick, what are you doing to me?"

"I don't know," he answered honestly. He stood there, inhaling that perfume, his mind rocketing to the past, wanting to kiss her so damned bad. Then, with a sigh, he let her go and rounded to his side of the car. He got inside, put the Ford in gear. Neither of them said anything as he drove out of the fairgrounds and across Lawford to a small jazz club on the north side of the downtown area. When he stopped the car, Carolyn turned to him and smiled. "You remembered."

"I did."

He hadn't forgotten much at all about Carolyn, as much as he'd tried. He still knew her favorite type of music. Her favorite meal. The scent of her perfume, and most of all, how she would feel in his arms and in his bed.

That, most of all. But even he knew a relationship couldn't be built on attraction. If it could, they'd still be together. Three years ago, they'd missed laying the foundation, and he wondered if it was possible to find the building blocks they needed this far after they'd undone what little of a relationship they'd had.

He came around the SUV and opened her door, taking her hand as she stepped out of the vehicle and onto the sidewalk. He didn't *need* to take her hand—he knew Carolyn was the kind of woman who could take care of herself and didn't expect him to be a gentleman—but he took her hand because he wanted to touch her, and not let go. Electricity sizzled between them, with a low hum of awareness. Again the desire to kiss her rose in Nick. But he knew if he did that now—

He wouldn't stop.

They entered the club, a cozy little place decorated in cranberry and gold. A trio comprised of a pianist, saxophonist and singer stood on the stage, singing an old Billie Holiday song. Only a few other people were sitting inside, so Nick and Carolyn had their choice of seating. They opted for a booth tucked in the back, providing privacy, a quiet little nook.

They hadn't been to this place in more than three years, but he remembered this booth. Remembered sitting across this very table from Carolyn, watching her laugh, sway along with the music. Remembered falling for her.

As if she could read his mind, her gaze broke away from his and she surveyed the room. "It's not very busy tonight."

"Probably because of the holiday. Most everyone went out of town." He studied her, reading the faint shadows beneath her eyes that spoke of exactly what Mary had told him—Carolyn worked far too many hours. She was, as she had been back in college, pouring herself into her career. They were still complete opposites. Nick, the guy who worked just enough to live and have fun, and Carolyn whose whole life was work. "Why are you in town? You could have gone off to some exotic island or a spa for the weekend."

"You know me. I don't do that. If I had my choice, I'd be in the office, working."

"You're still like that, Carolyn?" He'd hoped for more. He'd hoped she would have changed. That maybe he'd have had some influence on her.

"You say it like you're disappointed."

"I thought maybe…"

"Thought what? That I would get a life? Move on? Find someone else?"

The image of her with another man caused a surge of jealousy to wash over him. "No."

"You know why my job is important to me. Why I work so hard."

Because of what had happened to her father. Because she didn't want to let another murderer walk the streets. So she put in every hour she could to ensure no crime was left unprosecuted, no piece of evidence missed. "Your father wouldn't want you to spend your whole life behind a desk, either, Carolyn."

She turned away and he knew he had hit a nerve.

"So, what can I get you folks?"

The waitress's friendly voice interrupted them. She stood at the side of the table, a dozen gold bracelets jangling on her skinny wrist as she poised her hand over the order pad.

"Cosmo, with a lime twist."

"Dewar's on the rocks," Nick said. "And thank you, Regina," he added, reading her name tag. "It must not be a very busy night tonight for you."

She shrugged. "I kind of like it this way once in a while. Lets me rest up for those crazy Friday nights when it seems I run off twenty pounds between here and the bar."

Nick laughed. "We'll do our best to keep your bar running to a minimum so you get a chance to put your feet up."

The other woman grinned. "Thanks. I think you'll be my favorite customer all week." She gave Nick a friendly tap with the order pad, then headed off to the bar.

Carolyn's gaze swiveled back to Nick's. "How do you do it?"

"How do I do what?"

"Make friends with everyone. The kids. The waitress. Jean. And I'm this major social misfit."

"You're not a social misfit."

"Nick, those kids barely said three words to me at the picnic. I only got Bobby to talk to me when I was winning him a prize. You were the one all the children wanted to hang around with. You're their buddy. I'm just the fifth wheel that they put up with because they had to."

"Aw, Carolyn, you're not that bad."

She arched a brow.

"Well…" He hesitated. "You might want to try not using multisyllabic words like *reconvene* and *celebration*." He shrugged. "Just loosen up a little."

Carolyn groaned and dropped her head into her hands. "I was totally awful, wasn't I?"

"Not totally…" Nick paused. "Okay, yeah."

"It's just so hard for me."

In college, Nick had seen Carolyn—the stuffy Bostonian—and seen a woman he thought just needed to relax. Learn to be spontaneous. But now as he looked into her eyes and saw the glimmer of tears, the strain of how hard she had tried today written in her tensed muscles, her worried features, he realized her struggle to connect with people didn't stem from which side of the country she'd been raised on, but from all the facets of her background brought together.

"Aw, Carolyn, don't let it bother you so much. You're doing fine."

She arched a brow of disbelief.

"Was it always this hard for you?"

"Yeah, I guess." Carolyn toyed with her napkin. "It was so hard to fit in, being the only kid in my class who was an orphan, and the only one whose parent's murder had been all over the news. Then, on top of that…"

"You lived with an aunt who made antisocial into an art form."

"I survived."

Nick reached across the table and peeled her fingers away from her napkin, taking her hands again in his, wishing he could make everything easier for her. Wishing she would let him be Sir Galahad and knowing that was exactly the opposite of what Carolyn Duff wanted. "I know you did, Carolyn. I know. But it was still hard."

She had survived—and thrived. Built strength on top of her scars.

"It's just…I forget how to be a kid, if I ever really knew. I'm so uncomfortable around them."

"They don't bite, you know." He pretended to think about that for a second. "Most of them, anyway."

Carolyn laughed. "What's the secret?"

Just the reward he'd been looking for—

Carolyn's smile. "It's easy. Just think of the most immature thing you can. And then say it or do it. Works for me."

Another smile crossed her face, blasting Nick with a beam of sunshine. Damn, when she smiled, he had a hard time remembering his own name.

"Nick, you lived like that. I never did. I had to grow up too fast. And you…"

"I had the apple pie childhood."

But how had all that apple pie benefited him? He'd had it easy, really, and in turn become the easy, fun-loving guy. The one who hadn't really realized how much he wanted something more—

Until he'd had it for a second, then lost it.

Was there a chance of getting it back? Or should he simply learn his lesson once and for all, and accept what was and wasn't in the cards?

"Me, I lived with Aunt Greta," Carolyn went on, "who made Mommie Dearest look warm and fuzzy."

The waitress came back with their drinks and dropped them off, sending a smile Nick's way. "Here you go. I made sure the bartender gave you a little extra."

"Thank you."

"Oh, it serves me, too," she replied. "Saves me a trip back."

Nick chuckled as the waitress headed away.

Since no one else had entered the club, she slipped into a booth with another waitress and the two of them started chatting.

He returned his attention to Carolyn. "You can connect with these kids if you want to, Carolyn. All it takes is opening up. You did that before."

"That whole opening up thing is easier said than done." She shrugged. "Look at you. You have an instant friend in the waitress, for Pete's sake."

"You have friends. Mary, for instance."

"I do, but it's harder for me. I just don't do this as easily as you do."

"Because….?"

"Because I missed something in Friendship class." Carolyn smiled, then took a sip of her drink and shook her head. "I don't think I did the homework."

"You made friends with me."

"*You* were different."

"How? What made me different?" Maybe, if he could reassemble the pieces of their relationship, see where it fell apart, he could insert the missing parts. Make it work again. With time, could they be together again?

Would it be better the second time around?

Looking at her now, feeling like he could drown in those emerald-green eyes, he wanted it to be better. Wanted it to work. Wanted to prove to her that he had changed, become a different man than the one she remembered from college. Wanted to take her in his arms and promise her—whatever it took, whatever she wanted.

"You made it so easy, Nick. Just like you do with everyone."

If he was so good at making people like him, why couldn't he have made her fall in love? He realized now, with the passing of time, that they'd rushed into marriage, some kind of heady without-thinking decision that hadn't been based on love at all, just a powerful cocktail of infatuation and lust.

If he'd given their relationship more depth...

Where would they be now?

He shook his head. "It wasn't me. It was you."

"Me?" She toyed with the rim of the martini glass. "Your memory is a little faulty."

"I'm serious, Carolyn. There was something about you. Something that made it so easy for me to be myself. But I don't think I ever really opened up, not like I should have."

"Nick, you're one of the most open people I know."

He picked up the scotch, knocked a little back. "I'm not. Not really. Not with most people. I talk, yes. I joke. But...I don't *really* talk. I haven't buckled down and gotten serious about anything besides my career, and even that hasn't been as satisfying as I expected it to be. I never even got that serious about us."

"No, you didn't." Crimson rose in her cheeks and she dipped her gaze to study her drink.

Guilt sat heavy on his chest. "I'm sorry, Carolyn."

"It's okay, Nick. It's in the past."

"Yeah. Where it should stay, right?" His breath held while he waited for her answer, even as he knew he shouldn't. Getting involved with Carolyn again would probably be a mistake. Had he changed all that much? Really?

No.

Could he honestly give her now what he hadn't been able to give her then?

No.

Then why wrap himself in the same mistakes… knowing they'd have the same outcome? Because he'd gotten distracted by the feel of her in his arms, the scent of her perfume, the very nearness of her.

"Why did you really do it, Carolyn?"

There was no need to explain what he was asking, because they both knew the real question. The massive elephant nobody had wanted to discuss, but had been sitting on the table between them all this time. They'd talked around it for days, but neither had wanted to poke at the beehive that had been their divorce.

Well, Nick was tired of letting it lie dormant. He wanted to rile up the hive. See what happened. Because, despite everything, despite knowing he was better off without her, he still wanted Carolyn—and if there was any chance that she still wanted him, too, he was willing to put up with feeling that sting again to see where it might lead.

"You know why. Because Ronald Jakes got out of jail again. Those idiots on the parole board thought he was rehabilitated. That a few years in jail without any trouble meant he was safe to let loose on the public. But he wasn't," Carolyn said, studying the drink again, as if it were a crystal ball to the past. "I couldn't stay with you and pretend to be happy while he was out there, going after someone else."

The band segued into a popular Frank Sinatra compilation. Their waitress got up to refill another table's drinks, then sat back down. But at the booth where Nick and Carolyn sat, the tension tightened.

"But once he was caught again, back in jail for good, Carolyn, why didn't you come back? Why couldn't we have tried again?"

That was the question she had never answered. She had used the parole and reoffending of Ronald Jakes, her father's murderer, as an excuse to let their marriage slip away, and never fought to reclaim it. The weeks had passed, turned into months, then years, and Nick kept thinking that one of these days Carolyn would turn around, rethink her decision. He'd given her time, space, all the things he thought she needed, and then realized he'd given her so much time and space—

She wasn't coming back.

"Why didn't *you* come after me, Nick?" She met his gaze with her own. Clear, direct and honest. "You don't have to answer me, because we both know why. We rushed into a marriage, but neither of us were ready for what being married entailed. Buying a house, having kids. Look at us." She gestured between them. "We can barely handle taking a kid to a fair for an afternoon. Never mind a lifetime of that. You're not so bad at it, but if anything, these last couple of days have shown me how un-apple pie I am."

"The way you grew up doesn't have to dictate how you live the rest of your life."

"Don't be giving out advice when you're not following it yourself."

He sat back in his seat. "What is that supposed to mean?"

"You're still acting the way you did back in college. You're not growing up. You're not settling down. It's all a game." She let out a gust. "*I* was part of the game."

He leaned forward, caught her hands. The cozy

restaurant provided a dark, intimate cover, leaving them nearly alone, while the sultry jazz music played on in the background. Her breath fluttered in and out, her pulse ticked in her throat, and no matter how frustrated he got, all he could think about was kissing her, damn it. "You were not."

"Oh, yeah? Tell me the truth, Nick." Carolyn closed the distance between them even more. "Did you want me because I was a challenge, that cold Bostonian girl who turned down every guy at Lawford U, or because I was truly someone you loved?"

"I…"

She tugged her hands out of his grasp, grabbed her purse and slid out of the booth. She paused by the table. "Just the fact that you're hesitating answers the question."

Then Carolyn left. Something in her broke as the door shut behind her, muting the sound of the music. And Nick.

Carolyn stood on the sidewalk, waiting for a cab. She inhaled the warm, humid summer night air. A slight buzz of traffic filled the streets around her. A few cabs passed, but all had their lights off. Occupied.

The door to the club opened, releasing a burst of air-conditioned air, a snatch of a song. And Nick.

"You think that settles it?" he asked. "You think

the only reason I wanted you was to add some kind of silly conquest to my list?"

"Yeah." Now that she had said it, the truth became a sharp edge slicing along her heart. She'd thought she couldn't hurt over Nick Gilbert anymore. She'd been wrong.

"I wanted you for a hundred different reasons, Carolyn. And I still do."

"Nick, there's nothing between us except past history." She turned back toward the street. Where was a cab when you needed a really good exit?

"Nothing, huh? Why don't you try this for nothing?" Then before she could react or think, Nick took her in his arms and pulled her to him.

And kissed her.

Three years had passed since the last time she had been kissed by Nick Gilbert, but it felt like three hundred. Carolyn's entire body surged forward, responding like a starving traveler who'd stumbled upon a feast. Her arms reached around him, locking in on familiar muscles and planes, fitting into the same places as before, drawing him closer. Closer still.

His lips knew hers as well as the musicians inside had known their notes. At first his mouth drifted over hers, soft, easy, gentle—a prelude to what was to come—then, with a note of urgency, his hands splayed against her back and his mouth opened against hers. And everything within Carolyn opened in return.

He tasted of scotch and old memories, of everything she had denied herself over the past three years, and everything she had dreamed about and ached for, when the regrets crept in and shared her bed at night. Her fingers slid into his hair, then down his neck, along his shoulders, as if she couldn't get enough of touching him now—

As if she knew she'd better memorize this kiss because there wouldn't be another.

Nick pulled back, but his arms remained holding her tight to him. "*That's* what we still have in common, Carolyn. And if you'd start with that, *then* we could move forward."

She swallowed hard. How easy it would be to let that kiss be enough. To pretend everything was fine. But she knew better. And in her heart she knew Nick did, too. "It wasn't enough then, Nick. And it's still not enough. I wish it was. Oh, how I wish it was."

He broke away, a gust of frustration escaping him. "What is it with you and these emotional walls? Getting close to you is like trying to scale Alcatraz."

She looked at the man she once thought she'd known better than herself and realized she'd been wrong. It had taken two to end this relationship—and it was now taking two to keep it from blossoming again. "Don't talk to me about putting up walls, Nick Gilbert. Not when you've thrown up just as many emotional bricks as I have."

A cab came down the road, its top light on, and Carolyn raised her hand. In the kind of luck that only seemed to happen in the movies, the yellow cab stopped, Carolyn got in and left.

Before she could be wrapped in Nick's spell again.

CHAPTER EIGHT

JEAN'S face said it all. But Nick still forced himself to ask the question. "Where's Bobby?"

"He can't come today. We're looking for a temporary placement for him." A heavy sigh escaped Jean, seeming to weigh down the air around all of them.

Not that the air had been all that light to begin with. As promised, Carolyn had arrived at the city park where the best fireworks viewing could be found, but hadn't said much to Nick. They had planned to spend the late afternoon at the park, have a picnic dinner, then let Bobby play before the fireworks started late that night. Nick wondered how they were going to get through all that time with him and Carolyn barely speaking, because it seemed pretty clear they'd gone back to being—what was her word?—cordial colleagues.

"A temporary placement?" Carolyn asked. "Why?"

"His mother had to be admitted to the hospital this morning. She's not doing well. They think she has pneumonia, and after just battling breast cancer, the doctors didn't want to take any chances, so they had her checked in."

Carolyn put a hand to her heart. "Is she going to be all right?"

"The doctors think so. And she'll probably only be there for a few days, at most. She needs an IV, some antibiotics. She's been feeling ill for a while but resisted going to the hospital because she didn't want Bobby to be put into foster care again."

"I understand that," Nick said. "It's clear how much she loves him."

Several other families passed by, heading for the small public barbecues set up by the picnic tables. The scent of grilled meat filled the air, coupled with the sound of laughing children and barking dogs.

"Right now," Jean said, "Bobby's at a residential child care facility, until I can find him a foster family. It's a holiday weekend, so I'm having a hard time. Everyone's away on vacation."

"But surely, you have lots of families to choose from."

Jean indicated the picnic table beside them and gestured for the two of them to sit. "Can I be frank?"

Nick and Carolyn nodded in tandem and settled onto the opposite bench.

"We don't have a ton of foster parents to choose from. There's a long program to go through to be approved. Finding a temporary home at the last minute, especially on a holiday weekend, can be a challenge." Jean placed a hand on Carolyn's, met Nick's gaze. "I don't want you two to worry about Bobby. We'll find someplace for him until his mother is out of the hospital. He'll be fine."

"But what if you don't?" Carolyn said.

Jean's eyes were sad, filled with a reality she knew, but didn't really want to share. "He'll stay at a residential facility. It's not our first choice. And the upheaval for Bobby has already been so hard."

"Isn't there any other option?" Nick asked. He thought of Bobby's eyes, of the sadness he had seen in the boy's face. Damn, that kid had already faced enough. When would he catch a break?

"Well..." Jean paused. Looked from one of them to the other. "Bobby's mother and I did discuss one other possibility. And I wouldn't bring it up if I wasn't completely out of options."

"What?" Carolyn and Nick said at the same time.

Jean steepled her fingers. "Bobby responded really well to the two of you. He *smiled*. He *laughed*. You have no idea how huge that is. This is a boy who has had nothing but tragedy for the last year of his life. His mother liked the two of you. She said Bobby did nothing but talk nonstop about the picnic and the fair."

"We had a great time with him, too. He's a fabulous kid," Nick said.

"He is," Jean agreed. "Pauline said she hasn't seen her son this happy in ages, and she'll do about anything to keep him that way, especially while she's in the hospital."

"I can understand that," Nick said. He thought of his own mother, how she'd put her family ahead of virtually everything. The Gilberts had been blessed with a happy home, free of what Bobby had gone through, but they had one commonality—mothers who deeply loved their children.

Jean bit her lip, then went on. "Because of that, she'd much rather see him stay with friends than strangers."

"Friends?" Carolyn asked. "As in…?"

"You two."

The words hung in the air. No one said anything for a long moment.

"You want *us* to watch Bobby?" Carolyn said.

"It's an idea."

Carolyn's gaze met Nick's. Held. They each knew how being in a foster home had affected Bobby. They'd seen it in the boy's eyes. Heard it in his voice.

Carolyn thought of her own childhood. Of

being ripped out of the only home she'd ever known, and being sent to live with a cold, dictatorial woman, essentially a stranger, who had never extended a warm hug or a kind word. What difference would it have made to her to have had even a few days with someone who had made her laugh? Made her smile? Given her the memories of potato sack races and cotton candy?

Would she have been able to forget what had happened to her father, if only for a little while, and felt like a normal child? Could it be possible to give that same gift to Bobby?

"Are you thinking what I'm thinking?" Carolyn asked Nick, wondering whether she could even do this, because this was completely not her area of expertise. *Out of her comfort zone* didn't even begin to describe it. "I mean, it's a crazy idea, but you said before, you and I are better— "

"Together than apart," he finished, reading her mind, slipping into the familiar patterns from three years ago as if no time at all had passed. "It's only a few days. I'm sure we could do it."

"I can rearrange my work schedule." Carolyn smiled, suddenly feeling like this was the perfect choice. Helping Bobby—what better way was there to spend her time? "Mary would be thrilled to help me do that."

"I'm owed some vacation time on my end, too."

Even as the plan took place between them, Nick couldn't believe they were considering such a crazy idea.

But then he thought of Bobby. Of the wonder he had seen in the boy's face over simple things like a stuffed dragon, a ride on the Ferris wheel, a new truck. He'd appreciated everything—and asked for nothing.

Nick had been so incredibly fortunate in his own life. This would be a chance to give back, and see a direct result of his efforts. He'd enjoyed the toy buying, the picnic, the fair, so much more than he had expected. He looked to Carolyn again and nodded.

"Jean," Carolyn began, "Nick and I would like to take Bobby in, until it's time for him to return to his mother."

Then an awful possibility occurred to Nick. What if Pauline never got better? What if Bobby eventually had to leave and go into permanent foster care? Could Nick let him go then?

He'd have to. He certainly couldn't take Bobby on as a son. Nick was a single man—a man who worked an incredible amount of hours—a man with few responsibilities, who hadn't even managed to hold on to a marriage. Heck, he'd barely grown up himself.

Clearly, he wouldn't make a good father, and especially not a good single father. Surely, if something tragic were to happen, Jean would find someone to take Bobby. Someone who would love him and want to give the boy a permanent home.

"I was only throwing the idea out. You two don't have to do this," Jean said. "It's a terrible imposition, on such short notice, and—"

"We want to," Nick said, thinking again of the boy and of the way his face had lit up at the fair, of how a simple thing like winning a stuffed toy had changed his outlook for hours. "That way, he can still go to the fireworks, still have the fun that we promised him, and his mother won't have to worry. He'll be in a stable home, with two people."

Relief flooded Jean's features. "Are you really sure?"

Once again, Carolyn and Nick locked gazes. An electric thrill of connection ran between them, hot, fast. This was what had brought them together in law school, this energy, this shared passion for changing the world. They each nodded, then turned back to Jean. "Yes, we're sure," Carolyn said.

"Forgive me for getting personal," Jean said, "but you two aren't married and…don't live under the same roof. How are you going to make this work?"

Ah, the one detail they had overlooked in their rush. They'd both only been thinking of the child, not each other. In that moment, Nick saw Carolyn realize what their hasty offer entailed—the two of them being together.

Entirely together. Under one roof. For the next few days.

It had only taken them three weeks the last time they'd been together on a continual basis to make the decision to run off and elope. How long would it take, the second time around? Or would they realize this time in a matter of days instead that they were meant to continue on their separate paths?

"We'll figure it out," Carolyn said. "For Bobby's sake."

"Of course we will," Nick added. But at that moment, with every one of his senses on heightened Carolyn alert, he wasn't sure what he was supposed to be figuring out—

How to love Carolyn again, or how to forget her again.

The overnight bag sat in the foyer, a blaring announcement of Carolyn's insanity. She stared at the small brown suitcase, wondering if it was too late to back out. To come up with another plan.

Then she thought of Bobby and reconsidered. Hadn't she known what it was like to be shuffled off to someone she didn't know, someone who didn't really want her?

For him, she could do this. She'd just avoid

Nick. Not look at him when he woke up in the morning, his hair slightly mussed from sleep. Steer clear when he stepped out of the shower, his skin warm and steaming from the heat. Keep an entire floor between them when he went off to bed and sank beneath his covers, wearing—

"Do you want me to show you to the guest room?"

Nick's voice, low, husky, behind her. Carolyn tensed, then relaxed, steeling herself again before turning around. She would not react. Would not show him that hearing his voice, seeing him here—in the most intimate of environments, his home—had any affect whatsoever on her.

Whoa. He looked good. Wearing only a simple blue cotton T-shirt and cutoff shorts. His feet were bare, the muscles of his arms exposed, and the tattoo, that silly shark tattoo, peeked out from under the sleeve, teasing at the edge of her vision.

Bandit skidded in, plopped down beside his master, then nosed forward, sniffing at the new guest. He offered up a slobbery greeting on Carolyn's hand, then sat back and panted happily. She'd won the dog over with nothing more than a smile.

"Sorry, I'm a mess," Nick said, grabbing a towel from the counter and wiping his hands. "I was doing a little yard work before you got here.

Trying to clean up out there so Bobby will have some room to play. The weather's so nice and—" He cocked his head, studied her. "What? Do I have grass in my hair or something?"

"Oh, oh, no." Shoot. She'd been caught staring at him. Well, what woman in her right mind wouldn't? Nick Gilbert gave *handsome* a new definition. And it had been way too long since she'd been on a date. "I just got lost in my thoughts."

He took a step closer. "Were any of those thoughts about me?"

He knew she'd been staring at him, darn it. "No," she lied.

"Too bad. Because a few of mine lately have been about you." Another step closer.

"Just a few?" she said, trying to tease, but the words just sounded panicked.

He caught the strap of her sundress beneath his finger and Carolyn froze, unable to think, to hear, to do anything but stare into Nick's eyes and think about those few days they had been married. How wonderful the days had been. How much sweeter the nights had been. His touch was light, almost chaste, yet the sensation of skin on skin sizzled along her nerve endings, sparked her memories.

Had it been this good three years ago? No, this was better. Hotter. More tempting. Because she *knew*. She knew what pleasure awaited her in Nick's arms.

"I've had more than a few thoughts about you," he said, his voice low and dark with a mirror of her desire. "In fact, every other thought ever since that kiss outside the jazz club has been about you. Maybe we shouldn't have agreed to move in together. Even for a few days." Another step, closing the gap. "Why can't I forget you, Carolyn?"

"Uh, because you once told me that you have a photographic memory?" The words were a squeak, her senses off-kilter, her normal equilibrium gone. Good thing she'd never faced Nick in court, because she'd have lost every time.

"Maybe," he said, his voice lower, darker now. "Or maybe it's because I never forgot this." And then he leaned down and kissed her.

This kiss wasn't like the one last night. It wasn't sweet, it wasn't quick. It didn't tease her, or make her wonder where they stood.

This kiss rocked her to her very core, and stamped every cell in Carolyn's body with the message that Nick Gilbert still wanted her. He cupped her jaw, then opened his mouth against hers, tasting her, holding her captive with the desire that still ran so strong in her veins that ignoring it would surely have made her fall apart.

Her arms circled around his back, her fists

bunching the cotton of his T-shirt, lifting the fabric until she could touch his back, feel his warm skin against her palms once again. She ran her hands up those hard planes, tracing the ridges of his spine, then over the tips of his shoulder blades, down again, over every inch of his skin. She had missed him. Missed this. Missed everything about Nick.

Nick's kiss deepened and he groaned, then his hand slipped between them and cupped her breast. Every one of Carolyn's senses erupted into a fire that had been lying dormant for so long—too long—and she arched against him, pressing her breast deeper into his palm. His name slipped out of her mouth, half moan, half whisper. Nick's other hand tangled in her hair, fingers dancing along her neck.

The grandfather clock in the hall gonged the hour and Nick pulled back, his fingertips sliding around and releasing her jaw last, as if he wanted to linger there for as long as he could. Then he smiled. "I think about *that* most of all."

"Me, too." Why bother lying? He'd only read the truth in her eyes, the quickening of her pulse, her rapid breathing.

He studied her, his eyes dark. "If we're going to stay here together, we might want to have a few ground rules."

"Ground rules?"

Nick traced along the edge of her lips. "Because if we keep doing that, I'm going to break every rule of gentlemanly conduct known to man, and with a child around, that's probably not a good idea."

Carolyn took a step back. Putting some distance between them helped her clear her head, find her footing again. "You're right. Bobby will be here in a few minutes, and although we want to be one big happy family for the next few days, we don't exactly want to go too far."

"Or pretend to be something we aren't." Nick's gaze met hers, penetrating, searching for answers. "Like happily married."

The truth. Right smack-dab back between them again. Why did they always have to circle back to this?

The dog, apparently disappointed that none of this concerned him, turned around and left the room, picking up a plastic bone as he left. He gave the toy a squeak-squeak of indignant protest at being left out of all the fun.

"You're right," Carolyn said, picking up her bag. All business again, any trace of what might have been between them a moment ago gone. Nick had a point. Pretending to be happily married—or pretending to be any kind of couple at all—could only lead to trouble and broken hearts down the road.

Where did she expect their kisses to go, really? After Bobby went home, she and Nick would return to their lives, to their careers. The impasse they had reached three years ago still as wide as ever. Nick was still the devil-may-care playful guy he'd always been, the one who couldn't see how important Carolyn's career was to her. He hadn't listened to her then; he wasn't listening to her now.

And either way, they wanted different things from their futures. Nick came from a large family. He'd told her that someday he wanted the same thing for himself. The three-bedroom house she stood in was in-your-face evidence of that. She was still the woman who wouldn't take that chance, partly because of the hours she worked and partly because she was no good at mothering. If ever two people weren't meant to be together, it was Carolyn and Nick.

"Maybe I should just get settled in," Carolyn said, "and then, when Bobby comes, we can concentrate on him. And forget that kiss ever happened."

His jaw tensed. "We're very good at that, aren't we, Carolyn? Pretending things never happened between us."

Before she could answer, Nick took the suitcase out of her hand and charged up the stairs.

CHAPTER NINE

THE trouble with acting on impulse was where it got you. All Nick could think about now was the way Carolyn had felt in his arms. How she had moved against him, touched him, kissed him back. How for one long, sweet moment she had been his again.

And then reality had intruded and brought them right back to square one. Fellow attorneys who used to be married. Now she was using the convenient Bobby wall to keep from even coming near him. Everywhere they went, it was Nick-Bobby-Carolyn, so that Carolyn didn't even have to get close to Nick.

Fine. That was probably just as well. He didn't need to court temptation more than once to know it was a bad idea.

They were at the park with Bobby, killing time until the fireworks started. The minute Bobby had arrived, Carolyn had announced that they should have a picnic at the park, as if she wanted to get out of the house as quickly as possible. They'd packed up a cooler with some food, grabbed a blanket and set out for the park, leaving a dejected Bandit at home.

Now, with the food eaten, Nick had put the cooler back in the truck and they were wandering the park, looking for the perfect location to view the fireworks. The sun had nearly set, casting everything around them in a dark-purple haze of twilight.

"I missed the fireworks last year," Bobby said quietly as they walked down a grassy hill. "That was when my daddy died."

Nick and Carolyn exchanged a glance. He saw tears well in Carolyn's eyes—of sympathy? Of understanding? Or of her own memories? She looked away first, and he wanted to reach out to her, but again she withdrew, putting up that damned wall.

Instead, Nick laid a hand on Bobby's shoulder. "Let's hope these fireworks are extra great." It was a wonder the words even made it past the lump in Nick's throat.

Bobby nodded. He thought for a minute, then he turned to Carolyn. "Do you think my dad can see them, too? In heaven?"

She seemed taken aback by the question. A shadow washed over her face.

She had to be wondering the same thing. Was her father watching from above? Had he watched all the milestones in her life? Her graduation from law school? Her first case? Her short-lived marriage?

How lucky Nick had been to have a two-parent cheerleading team for everything he'd done, while Carolyn hadn't had anyone. She'd forged forward, essentially on her own, through all the milestones in life. No one sitting in a cramped seat in the too-hot assembly hall of the elementary school, a tissue pressed to a face, beaming with pride over a screechy rendition of "Hot Cross Buns." No one who would hang every A-plus test on the refrigerator front and center, layering the achievements one on top of the other with the pride only a parent could have.

Carolyn turned her face up to the sky, then met Bobby's inquisitive look. "I believe he can, Bobby. And I bet he has the best seat in the house."

"Yeah." Bobby smiled at the thought. He had on a brand-new USA sweatshirt that Nick had bought him from a street vendor, and wore a neon necklace around his neck—a Carolyn purchase. Nick had no doubt that before the night was over, Bobby would be decked out with at least one item from every vendor staked out around the park. "Do you think your dad watched them from heaven with you, too, when you were little?"

Carolyn fiddled with the fringe on the edge of the blanket in her arms. "I don't know, Bobby. I haven't watched fireworks since I was eight."

"Really?" Nick gaped at her. "Your aunt never took you?"

Carolyn shrugged like it was no big deal. "She didn't see the point. Thought they were a waste of the city's money. And the show was put on after my bedtime, anyway."

"But surely one night out of the year—"

"You had to know my aunt Greta, Nick. There was no 'one night out of the year' with her. Not for anything." The pinched look on Carolyn's face told him the subject was closed.

"I like to stay up late," Bobby said, interjecting a change of conversation with the timing only a kid could have. "My momma says it's okay, as long as I'm reading."

"What kind of stories do you like to read?" Carolyn asked, clearly grateful for the subject switch. Once again, treading anywhere near her past had her building up the walls so fast, Nick could practically hear the bricks knocking into each other.

Bobby shrugged, and for a second Nick thought he wouldn't answer, would refuse again to connect with Carolyn. Nick was about to intervene, when Carolyn started talking again.

"When I was a girl," she said, the memory leaving her lips in a quiet stream, "my father used to read me adventure stories. Books with pirates and lost treasures. Knights who had to slay fire-breathing dragons, things like that. Those were my favorites."

Bobby brightened. "I like those, too! I don't have very many, though. When my momma is sick, we don't get to go to the library because it's a long walk. And pirate books are expensive to buy. But it's okay. Sometimes I just make up pirate stories in my head."

Carolyn smiled. "Well then, tomorrow how about we go to the bookstore and buy you lots of pirate books? That should keep you busy reading for a long time."

"You will? Promise?"

She nodded. "Nick and I will read as many of them to you as you want, too. One of the things I did to pass the time when I was a girl was read. I still love reading."

"I can't wait!" Bobby grinned. "I love book-stores. And books."

"That's great."

Bobby's grin spread further. "Can I go play for a while? Until the fireworks start?" Carolyn and Nick nodded. Bobby ran off to the playground, swinging his arms and humming to himself.

When Bobby was gone, Nick closed the gap between himself and Carolyn. "I think you've made a buddy now."

"It was easier than I expected."

"I hate to say it, but—" he grinned "—I told you so."

"At least he'll have some wonderful memories to take home with him."

"Yeah. Memories and toys." That was all they could give the boy. It wasn't anywhere near what Nick had had as a kid, but hopefully it would be enough.

Carolyn watched Bobby head over to the playground, then begin to climb on the jungle gym. Only a hundred yards or so separated them, but a feeling of panic rose in Carolyn's chest. "Do you think he's okay? Not too far away?" She glanced around the park at the swarm of strangers. "I don't think there's enough security here."

"He's fine, Carolyn. Nothing's going to happen."

"Maybe we should call him back. There are an awful lot of people here. Do you see that guy over there?" She gestured with her head. "I think he looks suspicious."

"The one who is helping his daughter climb the monkey bars?"

"No, the other one. The one on the bench. Watching the kids. What's he doing?"

"Watching his own kid." Nick took Carolyn's hand, rubbing a thumb over the back. "It's okay. Not every human is a criminal. And besides, we're right here."

She shook her head, not convinced, her gaze darting from person to person, assessing every one of them as if she were a judge determining guilt or innocence. "Bobby's not ours. I couldn't bear it if something happened."

"Carolyn, look at me."

It took a lot of effort, but she tore her gaze away from the boy and turned toward Nick. "What?"

"Everything will be fine. What happened to you isn't going to happen to Bobby." He reached over, brushed a lock of hair out of her eyes. "When you learn to let go, you'll have a life, too. The one you've always deserved."

She shook her head and busied herself unfolding the blue plaid blanket in her arms. Nick grabbed the opposite end and helped her spread it on the ground. "It's not that easy, Nick."

"It's exactly that easy. It always was."

Carolyn settled on the blanket, back to watching Bobby, the concern etched again in her face. "You always thought so."

"What's that supposed to mean?"

She sighed. "To you, everything is black-and-white. One and one makes two. But for me there are other variables, things you never considered. I don't blame you, Nick. You can't consider what you haven't experienced."

His temper flared, a burst of leftover frustration from years before, rising to the surface. "I can't consider what you've never told me, either."

"I've told you everything about my past."

He let out a chuff. "You've told me like you were a witness on the stand, Carolyn. Relating facts in a case, not giving me your heart." He gestured toward Bobby, who was holding on to the bars and swinging back and forth. "You told Bobby more in the last five minutes than you ever told me."

She followed his line of sight, considering his words for one long moment. "I suppose you have to ask the right questions, Counselor, to get the right answers."

Nick swallowed hard. Had that been the problem? He'd never asked the right questions? Never delved deeply enough with Carolyn?

They didn't say anything for a while, just watched Bobby play. "He looks kind of like you, don't you think?" Carolyn said softly.

Nick glanced at the boy. A towhead, yes, but Bobby did have some similar features. Same eye color, lanky build. "A little, yes."

"It makes me wonder…" Carolyn cut off the sentence, shook her head.

"Wonder what?"

"Nothing. Never mind."

"Oh, no fair, leaving me in suspense. Here, let The Great Nick read your mind." He turned her toward him and placed a palm on her forehead. The whole thing started out as a joke, a tease—one of the parlor tricks he'd pulled a hundred times in college—but then, as he paused long enough to think of what Carolyn might have been thinking, the truth hit him hard. His palm dropped away. The tease left his voice. "You're thinking what if…what if we had a child. What if Bobby was…ours?"

"Of course not." She inserted some distance between them. "You know I'm not the kind of person who should have kids."

"Why?"

"You know why, Nick. I work a million hours a week, so that rules me out right there."

Nick settled on the blanket, pretending to watch Bobby slide down the slide, dart back to the steps, climb up again and make the swooshing trip down again. "And why is that, Carolyn? Your work schedule can be shifted, you know. There are plenty of attorneys who have families and careers."

"I'm fulfilled the way I am now."

"If you're so fulfilled, why did you kiss me back?"

"If you're so happy, why did you kiss me?" she countered.

He let out a laugh. "Always the lawyer. Answering a question with a question. Am I going to have to get a bailiff and a Bible, Miss Duff, to get a straight answer out of you?"

A burst of white light exploded over their heads, arcing outward in a scatter of stars. "The fireworks have started, Nick."

He caught her gaze, defiant, strong. Sexy. Despite everything, he still wanted her. "Yes, Carolyn, they most certainly have."

Carolyn tried to keep her gaze on the explosions in the sky, the vibrant colors blasting outward in heavenly flowers. But every time another bloom of sparks soared overhead, Carolyn found herself glancing at Nick. Thinking of their conversation—

And of where they were going as soon as the fireworks show was over.

Back to his house. Back together. After all she had done for the past three years to stay away from Nick Gilbert—away from the temptation of his eyes, his smile, his touch—she had offered *voluntarily* to spend the next few days with him.

Crazy, absolutely crazy.

The humidity draped around them like a thick, heavy blanket. Carolyn had worn a sleeveless shirt and shorts, as had Nick. What had been a great decision weatherwise, however, only gave her a heightened awareness of Nick. Despite their conversation, their differences, differences that seemed to get less and less resolved the more time they spent together, she couldn't stop thinking about kissing him earlier, and about what it would be like to kiss him again.

Beside them, Bobby went on watching the fireworks, completely enthralled and utterly unaware of the adult tension right behind him.

Nick's fingertips brushed against Carolyn's bare shoulder and she flinched, then turned, a thousand nerve endings standing at attention. "Just brushing away a mosquito," he said.

"Oh. Thank you."

"Anytime." That familiar grin, the one she could have drawn blindfolded, curved once again across his features, and something tripped inside her chest. The switch that was always waiting, as if the light inside her had gone dark years before, and now here he was, the only one who could turn it back on. "Anytime at all."

Now, she wanted to say. And the next second after that. And the one after that. But she didn't say any of those words. Instead, she returned her attention to the sky—

And didn't see a single thing.

"How do they make these?" Bobby asked her.

"Well…" Carolyn began, then stopped. "I don't really know. Nick?"

He took the opportunity to scoot closer, and Carolyn drew in a breath, so very aware of his presence, of how they made a little family, and how if she let herself, she could believe this was real, that they were real, and together again. "They're made out of lots of things, Bobby. Gunpowder makes them explode, but it's the colors that are the cool part. Certain colors are made by different chemical compounds. Blue comes from copper salts, for instance, gold from aluminum and magnesium."

"That's pretty cool," Bobby said. "So the people that do this job gotta know how to mix all those chemicals, huh?"

Nick nodded. "And especially how to light the fireworks safely."

"When I grow up, I'd love to have that job. It would kind of be like being a dragon."

Carolyn chuckled. "Yes, I suppose it would be."

"Except, my momma says I should go to college." He crinkled his upper lip.

"You should," Nick agreed. "And when it comes time, you look me up. I'll write you a recommendation. Help you find a good school."

"You will?" His eyes widened, the blast of red and green above reflecting in his gaze, his smile. Then his smile drooped and he dropped his head. "Maybe I will."

Carolyn could have read the body language from a mile away. Bobby had been disappointed so many times in his life he didn't want to put any hope into the future. He'd rather let the dream go now than hold on to it for the next dozen years and then find out Nick was only making an offhand comment—and didn't really mean it.

"Bobby—" Carolyn began.

"I want to watch the rest," Bobby said, then he turned back and tipped his head upward, wrapped again in the show in the sky.

The hall clock was chiming eleven when Carolyn entered Nick's dimly lit kitchen. She raided his refrigerator and assembled a midnight snack of cheese slices and fresh fruit. Nick had gone all out with Bobby's arrival. Considering virtually everything in the refrigerator was new, Carolyn suspected Nick didn't usually stock four different kinds of cheese, three kinds of grapes and every other type of fruit grown in the United States— and a few foreign countries, too.

As she loaded decaf grounds into the coffeepot and set it to brew, she thought about Nick. When she'd first known him, he'd seemed so easy to read, as clear as crystal. But now there were facets to him she couldn't read. Had she been wrong about him before?

Or had she only seen the surface Nick and not looked for the deeper man?

"How's Bobby?" she asked when Nick entered the kitchen.

"Still zonked out. He never woke up, from the minute we got in the car, and never even stirred when I carried him upstairs. He's all tucked in, and he's got that stuffed dragon right under his arm."

Carolyn laughed. "He's pretty attached to that thing."

"I think he's pretty attached to us."

"He is, isn't he?" Carolyn said. "Maybe we shouldn't have done this. Knowing he has to go back home and someday maybe go to other foster homes, if his mother gets sick again. We won't always be there for him, Nick. It's not like Bobby is a neighbor's puppy we can take back and forth whenever we feel like having him over."

"At least we're giving him some really fun moments that he'll remember. That's got to count for something, right?"

"It's not enough. Not nearly enough." She shook her head and paced a little.

"Carolyn, you worry too much. I'm sure Bobby will be just fine."

She wheeled around. "And you worry too little. You're doing it again."

"Doing what again?"

"Pulling out just when someone needs you most."

"I'm not doing that."

"You are. Just like you did with me." She shook her head. "You know, I was an adult. I handled it okay, but Bobby's a kid. Don't let him down."

He scowled. "I'm not planning on doing anything of the sort."

But she could see, in the way he turned away, how he put some distance between them, that she had nailed his intentions. Disappointment sank heavy in her gut. For once in her life, Carolyn didn't want to be right. "Maybe you're not, Nick. But just keep Bobby's needs at the top of your list. I know what it's like to be him."

"And what is it like, Carolyn?" Nick asked, taking a step closer, the gap between them narrowing in the small kitchen. "Tell me."

"You know. I've talked about my past often enough."

"Talked, but not *told* me much. You accuse me of not getting involved, but how can I do that when you don't let me in? You've only let me glimpse the inside of you, Carolyn."

Carolyn didn't answer him. Instead, she handed Nick a cup of coffee, then followed him as they walked through the kitchen and out to the screened porch. Bandit stayed behind, gnawing happily on a new chew toy.

Outside, the night birds called softly to each other, and far in the backyard, bugs hummed. The moon hung low over the trees, and stars sparkled in the sky, like leftover fireworks. "I don't understand you, Nick."

"What don't you understand?" He shot her a grin. "I'm a guy. I'm a pretty simple creature."

"Why do you own this huge house but have no kids of your own? You never married again."

He didn't say anything for a long time. The birds filled the silence with their own chatter. "I haven't found anyone I wanted to settle down with, and either way, I'm not exactly the settle-down kind. Despite my temporary record to the contrary."

"But…why buy the house? I mean, most people buy homes after they get married."

"Yeah, they do. I guess I did it all wrong, huh?" He shrugged. "I saw this place as an investment. It's in a great neighborhood, corner lot. Nice acreage. When it became available, it made sense to buy it. Someday I'll sell and make a tidy profit. Like I said, it's an investment, only with windows and doors."

"That's all?" It was the kind of logical argument a lawyer would make. Full of justifications, facts. But…it sounded so sad. So…empty.

"Yep. That's it."

"Why didn't you ever remarry?"

The question, coming out of left field, did what she had expected—surprised him. But Nick recovered quickly. Clearly, like her, he was used to questions that rocked the boat a little. "Same reason as you, I'm married to the job."

"Perjury is a crime, Mr. Gilbert."

"I wasn't aware I was on the stand."

"And I never thought you'd lie to me."

He turned away, cupping the mug in both his hands and straying to the screened windows, staring out into the deep darkness beyond them. "I'm not lying, exactly. Like you, I've chosen my job instead of a relationship."

"But why?" Carolyn said, coming up behind him, so aware of their closeness. Of them being alone. Of the intimacy of darkness. She caught the scent of his cologne, inhaled it into her lungs, breathed until it was part of her. Her hand reached out into the darkness of the porch, but stopped inches away from touching Nick. "That wasn't the way you used to be. I mean, you were never Mr. Career."

"It's the way I should be. I'm fine for this kind of temporary gig, but maybe I shouldn't do it on a permanent basis." He turned to face her, his catching a glimmer from the light inside. "In fact, I think it was best that we broke up."

"*Best?*" Even though she had been the one to

deliver the words across that diner table three years ago, hearing him say that now, stung in ways she hadn't expected. Her hand dropped away. Cold air invaded the space between them. "How can you say that?"

"How can you be so surprised? You know me, Carolyn. I might have tried my hand at it, but deep down inside, I'm not a commitment guy, a family man. I'm the guy who makes people laugh, the one who has a good time, then gets out before things become too serious. Right?"

"And is that what you're going to do here, with me? With Bobby?"

"Bobby staying here is temporary, though I'm sure we'll still see him afterward from time to time."

"You didn't answer me." Her gaze met his. Direct. Not allowing him room to escape. "Is that what you're going to do with me?"

"Isn't that what you want? Just like you did before?" He took a step closer. "You were the one who called it all off. You barely gave us a chance, Carolyn."

"And how would we have worked out, Nick? Now you're telling me that we would have come to the same destination regardless of what I said that day."

"We probably would have. Don't you agree?"

She wanted to scream in frustration. Nick

couldn't have been sending more mixed messages if he was a Morse code operator with broken fingers. "What is wrong with you? One minute you're kissing me, the next you're telling me the best thing we ever did was break up. What do you want, Nick?"

"What do *you* want, Carolyn? I can ask you the same thing you're asking me. You're here with me now, but why? Where do you see this ending?"

She saw the intensity in his gaze, how he sought hers for the truth, and knew she couldn't demand it from him without giving it in return. But was she ready to admit how she felt? Doing so would mean traveling a road she couldn't backtrack.

But, oh, how easy it would be to just give up this fight. To close the distance. Her heart raced, her skin tingled with awareness and her hand curled at her side, fingers itching to touch the bare skin on his arms, the exposed vee above his shirt.

Instead she took a step backward, into the shadows. "I'm here for Bobby."

"Perjury, Miss Duff," he reminded her.

"I'm not lying." Entirely.

"You're not here out of curiosity? To see what might have been?"

"Is that why you're here?" she countered.

A grin curved across his face. "Never have a love match between two lawyers. There are no answers, only one-upmanship in questions." Then he paused and met her gaze again. "Tell me the truth, Carolyn, where is this going?"

Nick's pulse ticked in his throat, a constant beacon, drawing Carolyn forward. She laid the coffee mug on a nearby table and closed the distance between them. The wildlife had gone so quiet, it seemed she could hear Nick's heartbeat— or was it hers? She could measure his every breath, hear her own escape in ragged jerks.

And then she stopped resisting, stopped fighting a battle she wasn't going to win, not while she and Nick were under the same roof. She reached out and touched him, her hand on his arm—warm skin, so warm—then his shoulder, then his neck, pulling him closer. "Maybe only here."

She leaned forward, raising on her toes and kissed him, because it was a lot easier to do that than to tell Nick the truth.

That she had already started falling in love all over again.

CHAPTER TEN

NICK didn't sleep.

He stared at his ceiling, then got up and paced the floors of his bedroom. Moonlight sent a slash of white across the hardwood floors.

He was in deep. Too deep.

In the morning he'd have to find a way out. Somehow he'd have to end things—sever the ties completely—with Carolyn. Find a way back to the life he'd had before, to a place with no commitment, no expectations. It was the only way to protect them both. To keep him from making the same mistake twice.

That day in the diner, when she'd left for Boston, it had taken him about five seconds to decide to go after her. He'd missed her in the airport and ended up on a separate flight. When he'd arrived in the city, however, he'd seen Carolyn in a different mode: the passionate, crusading spirit that would end up defining her career.

And he'd realized at that point that he would never be that serious about anything. That she was someone who dug in with both heels and held on tight. He had yet to find anything that mattered that much to him.

Back then, not even their marriage. They barely knew each other, had married on a lark. So he let her go. Didn't fight her on the divorce. He'd simply cleaned up the debris of their marriage and moved forward.

Carolyn was right. What had changed between them, really? He hadn't become any more serious now than three years ago. It was simply his own selfish heart still wanting her.

The best decision, Nick decided, climbing back into his bed, was to call it quits. Before anyone got in too deep. And hearts got broken.

Because his own was already beginning to ache.

On Tuesday morning the paper arrived with a slap on Nick's front porch. Carolyn retrieved it, thinking how odd it felt to wake up in his house. As she made a pot of coffee and opened up the paper, she decided she would tell Nick that this grand experiment was over.

What had she been thinking last night? Kissing him? Entangling them even more than they had been before?

Today she'd move out. She'd still be here during the day for Bobby, but at least remove herself from the temptation of spending every night in Nick's arms. Last night had been torturous. After that kiss, going to bed—without him—had been nearly impossible. She'd barely slept, acutely aware of his bedroom just down the hall. Worse, she'd been filled with the knowledge of what it had been like the few days they had been married. Her mind had teased her with images of how it could be again, if only she'd journey those few feet.

But no. Nick and she were as different as two people could be. He still didn't know her, still didn't listen. She'd reached out to him once during their marriage, asked for his help, asked for him to support her—

And he hadn't heard her. She couldn't risk her heart again. Only a fool did that twice when the answer was already there, right in front of her.

She redoubled her resolve. As much as she cared about Nick, the best decision was to walk away.

Nick entered the kitchen, fully dressed, with faint shadows beneath his eyes. Apparently she hadn't been the only one missing a few winks last night. "Good morning." He reached for the pot of coffee and poured himself a cup. "Thanks for making this."

"No problem." She sipped at the hot beverage, then decided to tackle the difficult subject before the day—and her courage—got away from her. "Nick, we need to talk."

Bandit, who had followed along behind his master, a squeaky bone in his mouth, heaved a sigh of long-suffering doggie patience and slid under the kitchen table. The bone dropped to the floor by his paws.

"I was about to say the same thing." Nick toyed with his mug. "This isn't working out."

"I agree. Us under the same roof—"

"Is too tempting."

"Especially when we both know it isn't going to lead anywhere."

"Are you sure, Carolyn?"

With one word she could undo this. She could be back in Nick's arms, just like last night. Longing ran through her, swift and painful, tempered by common sense. The urge to reach out, lay a hand on his shoulder and feel that strength beneath her palm, had her curling her fingers. "Yes, I'm sure."

This was what she wanted. What she had always wanted. She would be back at work in a few days, and all of this would be nothing more than a memory. Just like before.

A wave of regret washed over her. But she

brushed it off, forced it away. She had already survived a breakup with Nick once before. She could do it again.

She could.

The front door opened, which sent Bandit scrambling to his feet and running down the hall with a flurry of barks. In walked a man who looked like a younger version of Nick. "Knock, knock. I bet you forgot our golf game this—" He stopped short, one hand patting Bandit, his mouth agape, eyes wide, staring at her. "Whoa. You have company. I'll come back later."

"No, no, I'm not—" Carolyn felt her face heat "—company. I'm…Carolyn."

"*You're* Carolyn?" The other man stepped forward, a grin spreading across his face. "Well, hello. I've heard quite a bit about you. And I have to say, you are probably the last person I expected to see here, but—"

"My brother is going to shut up now," Nick interrupted, "if he wants to keep his jawbone intact."

The other man chuckled, then extended his hand. "I'm Daniel. The younger and cuter Gilbert son. And the one with all the manners, apparently."

Nick shot his brother a glare.

"Carolyn Duff," Carolyn said, shaking hands with Daniel. "And really, there's nothing going on here. Nick and I are just helping out one of the kids from the picnic, Bobby Lester. His mom is in the hospital for a few days and he has no other family, so she asked us to take him in. Nick and I being together is just a temporary partnership." Damn. She was babbling again. Take her out of the courtroom and she was a social mess.

Daniel arched a brow. "Temporary. Uh-huh."

"Didn't you have a golf game to get to?" Nick asked.

Daniel hopped over the side of an armchair and settled himself into the seat. "Kind of hard to play a golf match against myself. Besides, I'm not in the mood for golfing now. I found something much more interesting to watch."

Nick groaned. "You are a pain in the neck."

"That's what makes me kin," Daniel said, giving his brother a teasing grin.

Bandit began whining and running circles around Nick's feet. "The dog needs to go out. I'll be right back."

"Take all the time you need." Daniel waved Nick off. "I'll chat with Carolyn while you're gone. Bring her up to speed on all your bad habits."

Nick muttered a few choice words under his breath as he rounded the corner.

"Okay, so give me the straight scoop," Daniel said, turning to Carolyn. "Are you and Nick getting back together? Because without you, the man has been as miserable as a monkey in a pool."

Carolyn laughed. "No, we're not. This is just for a few days."

"I've seen the way you look at him. And the way he looks at you. What's stopping you from getting together?"

"For one, we're divorced. For another, Nick's looking for different things out of life than I am. He always has been." She shrugged as though it didn't matter. As if it didn't disappoint her that nothing had changed. "He's not the settling-down, getting-serious type and I'm…well, I'm as serious as an encyclopedia."

"Whoa, whoa." Daniel put up his hands. "Where did you get the idea that Nick isn't the settling-down type?"

Carolyn slipped into the second armchair and ran a hand over the faded tapestry pattern. "Daniel, everything about Nick screams not settling down. You know him."

"Well, yeah, I do. And granted, he's not exactly Commitment Charlie, but I like to think that's because he hasn't had enough incentive." Daniel gave her a knowing grin.

"Don't look at me. Nick and I already tried the marriage route and failed the test."

"You guys were students. Immaturity comes

with the territory." Daniel waved a hand in dismissal. "You should try it again now. Considering you're older and wiser."

"Exactly. We're older and wiser, which is why we shouldn't do this."

"Oh, please. You're both just scared."

"We're not scared. Just…smart."

Daniel glanced over his shoulder, then returned his gaze to Carolyn, his voice lower now. "Did you ever think that maybe the reason the two of you broke up had less to do with what you did or didn't have in common and more to do with what you two didn't talk about? You were only together for, what, three weeks? And I bet not a lot of talking happened in that time."

"Well, no…" Carolyn's voice trailed off and heat filled her cheeks. Then she realized Daniel might be right. That was where you got when you married a man you'd known for three weeks. You made a lot of assumptions and didn't work with a lot of facts. Because they had, indeed, probably spent more time exploring each other's bodies than minds.

She'd always thought they had broken up about her decision to put her career ahead of their marriage. Had she missed a piece of the puzzle? Given up too easily? "Why? What did he tell you about why we broke up?"

Daniel leaned back in the chair. "Not for me to say. You ask Nick, if you want to know. Seems to me, the real problem standing between you two is a lack of words." Daniel chuckled. "What do you know? Two lawyers who are talking *around* the problem instead of talking it *out*."

Bandit came skidding around the corner, panting, as if afraid he might have missed a little fetch while he was outside. A few seconds later Nick entered the room and sent a suspicious glance at his brother. "What were you two discussing?"

Daniel chuckled, then got to his feet and headed to the door. "See you on Thursday night, Nick?"

"Of course."

"And should I tell Ma to set an extra place at the table?" Daniel gestured toward Carolyn. "You'll make her year."

Nick scowled. "You were *leaving*, weren't you?"

They could still hear the sound of Daniel's laughter, even after the door shut behind him.

"Clearly I'm not the only one with a determined matchmaker butting into my love life," Carolyn said.

"He's usually not this bad. I think he's just trying to take advantage of his younger-brother irritability factor." Nick's gaze met hers, and for a second her heart seemed to stop. "I hope he wasn't too hard on you."

"No, not at all." She considered asking Nick about

what Daniel had told her, but then she heard the sound of footsteps on the stairs. Bobby was coming down. Deep conversations would have to wait.

Just as well. Because the answers might not be something she wanted to hear.

"Are you *sure* you've got this under control?"

Carolyn laughed. "Contrary to what you might think, I'm good at more than just practicing law."

Nick raised a teasing brow, but Bobby stood on the sidelines of the living room, beaming with cheer. "Okay."

Bobby had come downstairs, and instead of wanting breakfast right away, he'd asked immediately about the pirate books. Since the bookstores weren't due to open for a couple more hours, Carolyn had suggested they instead organize a treasure hunt. She'd made the two guys wait inside for fifteen minutes while she set everything up in the backyard.

"Okay, I'm ready." She handed Bobby a crudely drawn map on a slightly crumpled piece of paper. Bandit danced around Bobby's feet, almost as excited as the boy. "Your map, sir."

"Is it real?" His eyes were wide as he puzzled over the directions.

"The only way to know is to follow it." Carolyn leaned down and pointed at the different drawings on the paper. "You have to watch for all these landmarks and take the exact number of steps to get to the treasures."

"Treasures?"

"Yep. There's more than one." Carolyn grinned. "What's a good treasure hunt with only one surprise at the end?"

Bobby beamed. "Can I start now?"

Carolyn opened her mouth to say yes, then glanced down at the dog, his tail waving wildly. "Wait. There's one more thing you need." She reached into the box of supplies she'd gathered from inside of Nick's house earlier, and pulled out a bright-red bandanna. "You need a partner in crime." Then she bent over, tied the bandanna around Bandit's neck and gave the dog a pat.

"Oh, he looks so cool! Like a real pirate!" Bobby tugged on the cloth and gestured toward the map. "Come on, Bandit, we need to go find some treasure!" The dog yipped, and off the two of them went, heading for the first stop on the map, the elm tree at the back of the yard. Bobby stopped by the tree, then started measuring ten paces to the nearby shrub. Soon he was rewarded with the unearthing of a small yellow ball.

Nick sidled up beside Carolyn. "Wow. I'm impressed. How did you come up with all of this?"

"One thing I learned to do while I was at Aunt

Greta's was entertain myself." Carolyn leaned back against the patio table and crossed her arms over her chest. "I reread those pirate books from my dad over and over again and used to come up with all kinds of imaginary stories. Then I'd hide things all over the house and make maps for myself to find them later."

"I take it Aunt Greta never joined in?"

Carolyn chuckled. "No, definitely not. But…I think she supported me in her own way. I'd come home from school, and sometimes there'd be a little bag of toys. Small things, like jacks. Or crayons. And when I'd run out of drawing paper, there'd always be a new pad." Carolyn turned to Nick. "And every month, for years, there was a new pirate book. She never talked about my father. Never talked about what happened, and she wasn't the best parent. But those pirate books…" Carolyn smiled and a glimmer of tears showed in her eyes "—those pirate books made all of it bearable."

"They told you she cared. At least a little."

Carolyn nodded, mute.

Nick's arm stole around her, and he drew her against his chest. She pressed her face to the soft cotton of his T-shirt and allowed a couple of tears to dampen the fabric before pulling away.

"Ah, enough of the past. There's a pirate's

treasure out there," she said. "And a pirate to attend to, who seems to want our assistance." Bobby gave them a wave from his place by the swing. "Are you going to help me search, matey?" Carolyn put out her hand, a smile on her face, the fun Carolyn he knew and remembered firmly back in place.

He laughed, so damned glad to see this woman that right now he'd have followed her to the ends of the earth if she asked. "Aye, aye, captain."

The doorbell rang in the middle of waffle making. Nick was cooking, Carolyn was threatening to get the fire extinguisher, Bobby was laughing and Bandit was running yipping circles around them all, hoping to get lucky with the rejected burnt attempts at breakfast.

To Nick, it felt exactly like a real family. Ever since Bobby had come downstairs and they'd started the pirate game, Nick had forgotten exactly why he'd thought it was a bad idea to get involved with Carolyn again. In the past hour he'd seen a side of her he hadn't expected.

Heck, the whole last few days he'd seen other sides of her he hadn't even realized she had. And he was longing for more.

More laughter to fill his house. More waffles— as awful as they had turned out. More treasure hunts in the backyard.

Suddenly he didn't want to return to the way things had been before. He wanted only for it all to stay exactly the same as it was right now.

"At least Daniel didn't just walk in this time," Nick said. "How about we all go out for breakfast and give up on this?"

"I vote for that," Carolyn said, thrusting a hand in the air. "Bobby?"

"Me too! If we can bring home a doggy bag for Bandit."

"Of course." Nick chuckled, then left the kitchen, heading for the front door.

When Nick was gone, Carolyn started cleaning up the mess. Bobby slipped into place beside her, eager to help, scraping the remains into Bandit's bowl, then helping her put the flour, butter and milk away. "I think it's safe to say Nick isn't the chef in the family," Carolyn said to him, and Bobby laughed.

She froze. Had she just said those words? "In the family?" And why was she surprised? For a while there, they *had* felt like a family. A regular mother, father and child, sitting down for a breakfast on an ordinary day. She'd grown comfortable here, with Nick, with Bobby, and had, somewhere along the way, lost the severe, strict courthouse Carolyn, along with the pins that had held her hair in place. She'd relaxed. Had fun. Forgotten about the disasters that could be looming around the corner. And found, as Nick had said, that it wasn't as hard as it looked.

It had been…wonderful.

"Maybe we should only let Nick make cereal with milk," Bobby was saying. "And peanut butter sandwiches. And—"

"Good morning."

Carolyn stopped washing dishes and turned around. Jean stood in the kitchen, trailed by Nick, whose face held the downturn of disappointment. "Jean."

"Hi, Carolyn." Then she smiled and turned to Bobby. "Hi, Bobby. How's it going?"

"Great. We're making waffles. But they're terrible. So Nick is taking us to a restaurant and letting them make the waffles."

Jean laughed. "Sounds like a good idea."

"Can I get you some coffee?" Carolyn asked, and as the words left her, she realized how much she had become at home in Nick's house, if she was already playing hostess.

"No, I'm not staying. Actually, I came by to deliver some good news." She bent down to Bobby's level. "Your mom is home from the hospital. And she's ready for you to come home, too."

He popped out of the chair, eyes wide with excitement. "She is?"

Jean nodded, laughing. "Absolutely. And I've arranged for a home health aide for a few days so she doesn't wear herself out. Plus there'll be a visiting nurse stopping by to make sure she's healthy and following doctor's orders."

"I can go home, right now, and see her?"

"Absolutely."

"Let me get my stuff!" He started toward the stairs, then spun back. "Is that okay, Nick? Carolyn? I mean, I really wanted to get waffles, too, but she's my mom and she's been sick and I want to see her real bad."

How could Carolyn feel one iota of disappointment at that face? But she did. She didn't want him to leave, didn't want this perfect bubble to burst.

All these years, she'd gone without a family, and now for a few days she'd had one, as oddly assembled as it had been. To lose it again, as quickly as she'd gained it—

Hurt.

But she knew she couldn't be that selfish, not when Bobby was overjoyed at being reunited with his mother. She glanced over at Nick and saw he seemed to be working as hard as she was at holding a smile on his face.

"If it was my mom, Bobby," Carolyn said, meaning the words and trying hard to force cheer into her voice, for Bobby's sake, "I'd be rushing out the door, too. I'm so glad she's better."

He smiled. "Me, too."

"Here, let me help you pack," Nick said. The two of them went up the stairs, the little boy talking the whole way, his joy so clear it shone like the sun.

"Kids like him remind me of why I do this job," Jean said. "It's nice to see a happy ending once in a while."

"Do you think his mother is going to make it?" Carolyn asked.

Jean nodded. "Her doctor told her as long as she takes care of herself, she should be fine. She's young. She caught the cancer early. And she's got a lot to live for."

Carolyn cast a glance toward the stairs. "Yeah, she does." She was sure Pauline knew just how much, especially after losing her husband. Caroline offered up a silent prayer that the days ahead would be filled with nothing but happiness for Bobby and Pauline. Then she went back to the dishes because her vision suddenly seemed awfully blurry. "I hope it all works out for him."

"And what about you?" Jean asked. "How will the story end for you?"

"Me?" Carolyn loaded the dirty dishes into a sinkful of soapy water. "My story will just keep going on as it has. I'll go back to work, go back to prosecuting cases. Putting bad guys in jail. Doing my part to change the world."

"Have you ever considered you're trying to change the world from the wrong end?"

Carolyn dried her hands and turned to face Jean. "What do you mean?"

"You were obviously great at this. Maybe," Jean ventured, "if you became a social worker, you could change these children's lives, *before* they grew up and became part of the criminal justice system."

"Oh, no, I don't think—"

"Just think about it," Jean said. The telltale sound of little footsteps coming down the stairs echoed through the house, announcing Bobby's return. "Together, you and Nick have a magic touch with children. And that kind of magic doesn't come along every day."

Bobby was leaving. This little fantasy world was coming to a close. Carolyn might have been able to fool herself into thinking she could have this world, that she could make this work, but she needed to get real. These past few days had been temporary. A vacation from reality. Nick hadn't changed, hadn't become Mr. Two-Point-Five-Kids overnight, and neither had she, even if part of her had flirted with the idea for a little while.

The magic Jean had thought she'd seen between Carolyn and Nick was really all an illusion. And the sooner Carolyn accepted that, the better.

Empty.

The house seemed emptier than ever before. Nick stood in the kitchen, at a loss. He could go into the office—but he'd already taken the day off. He could call Daniel, but the thought of suffering through a golf game—and his brother's questioning—was too much.

Or he could go to Carolyn.

But she had run out of here, practically on Bobby's heels, pleading a heavy workload even though she'd already taken the day off. He'd known it had been much more than that. She was avoiding him. Avoiding being alone with him. Because whenever they were alone, all those unanswered questions from the past came bubbling to the surface.

He had what he wanted—his life back to the way it used to be. No one expecting anything of him. No one to be responsible to or for. He should be happy. Instead, a strange sense of loss kept invading his thoughts.

Bandit started barking and darted out of the kitchen. A second later the barks stopped and Bandit returned, sliding under the table for a ball.

Daniel brought up the rear. "Don't you ever answer your door? Or is Bandit the new butler?"

"You're awfully determined to get a golf partner today."

"No, I gave up on the golf game. I came by to borrow your jet skis. I'm heading to the lake with a few of the guys."

"Sure." Nick waved a hand in the direction of the garage. "Keys are on the hook."

"Whoa. You're just letting me take them? No questions asked? And no, 'Can I come to the party, too?'"

"I'm not in the mood for a party."

"Not in the mood for a party? You? Since when?"

Nick scowled. "Don't you have a lake waiting for you? And probably a date, too?"

A knowing grin spread across Daniel's face. "This is about Carolyn, isn't it? Speaking of which, where is she? And the kid?"

"The kid has a name—Bobby."

Daniel's grin only widened, which sparked Nick's temper even more.

"Bobby's mother came home from the hospital, so he went back to his own house. And Carolyn went to work. As usual."

Daniel let out a low whistle. "So she left you."

"She didn't leave me. She went to work."

"Uh-huh." Daniel swung one of the kitchen

chairs around and sat down, draping his arms over the back. "So, are you just going to stay here and be the grumpy dwarf or are you going to go make things right with her this time?"

Nick crossed to the coffeepot and poured himself and Daniel each a mug, then sat down at the table. "There isn't anything to make right."

"I don't understand why not. Just this morning you were doing the happy family thing. And doing it pretty well from what I could see."

"It was an illusion," Nick said. "Like the card tricks I did when I was a kid. We pretended we believed it for a little while, and it seemed real. But it wasn't. Now we both go back to our lives."

"Oh, and such great lives they were, too." Daniel rolled his eyes. "For the oldest one in the family, you can be pretty stupid."

"What was wrong with my life?"

"What was so *good* about it?" Daniel countered. "You live in this big empty house all by yourself. Like you want to get married again, have a family, but you're afraid to go after what you want."

Nick scowled and got to his feet. "I'm not afraid of anything."

Daniel just sipped at his coffee, silent.

His brother was good at that. Playing the silent card, waiting for Nick to fill the gap in conversation. Nick refused to play that game, refused to give Daniel the satisfaction. "Do you want some lunch?"

"Not especially." Daniel leaned back, stretched, patient as the Cheshire cat.

"Well, I do." He didn't—it was still too early for another meal—but Nick needed the distraction. He opened the fridge, the door practically bouncing off its hinges, pulling out ham, cheese, mustard. He grabbed a loaf of bread and slapped together a sandwich but didn't eat it. He tossed the butter knife into the sink and turned around. "I screwed up with Carolyn before. What if I do it again? I married her for all the wrong reasons, didn't think about what I was doing, then didn't take the whole thing seriously enough and lost her. What kind of idiot does that make me?"

"A pretty big one." Daniel grinned. "But what if you go for it…and you don't screw up? What if the best thing ever just walked out your door today and you lost her twice? Now that would make you an idiot of Guiness World Record proportions."

Nick ran a hand through his hair. "Is there a reason I keep you on my Christmas list?"

"Yeah, I'm always right."

Nick paced the kitchen, the sandwich untouched on the counter, his coffee growing cold.

"All my life I thought I didn't want to have a family. I grew up with all that, and figured once I was an adult, I'd finally have me time, you know? I'd wait until I was, oh, I don't know, Methuselah's age to have kids. But then, these last few days, I realized…"

"That the whole family thing is a little more fun than the bachelor life?"

"Yeah. Maybe."

"Then go for it. Take a chance. Dive headfirst into the marital pool again."

Nick put up his hands. "I never said I wanted to run off to the nearest church."

"Bawk, bawk, chicken-boy." Daniel rolled his eyes. "Go after Carolyn and quit being so damned scared that you'll make the same mistake a second time. Talk to her. You'd be amazed what can happen if you do that."

"It's not that simple, Daniel." Even Nick could hear the weakness of his protest.

Daniel shot to his feet. "Hell, yes, it's that simple. You're looking for something that does exist if only you'll take a chance. You've been playing it safe, my brother. Playing games instead of taking things seriously."

"I am not."

His brother shrugged. "It's your life. You want to waste it, fine. But you're letting the best thing that ever happened to you get away. Because you're being too damned stubborn." He put his mug in the sink. "Thanks for the coffee. One of these days you'll thank me for the advice."

His brother walked out the door. Bandit trotted beside him, a ball in his mouth. Ever hopeful. Just like Daniel.

Nick glanced around his kitchen, all neat and tidy again, the traces of Bobby and Carolyn erased. It was as if they had never been there. He put his mug in the sink, then, as he did, a piece of paper caught his eye.

He picked it up, flipped it over. The treasure map.

X marked the spot for the biggest prize. The one that had lit Bobby's face—an old book on dragons that Carolyn had found in Nick's study, along with a ship in a bottle Nick used to keep on the mantel. When Bobby opened the shoebox and found those two prizes, he squealed with the joy of someone unearthing a pot of gold.

What if Nick could see that look of joy every day—on his own son's face? And share that joy, as he had today, with Carolyn by his side? See her smile, so content, so relaxed, so full of joy. For that one moment, Nick had felt as if the entire world was perfect.

His finger traced along the dashes, weaving along the 2-D version of his backyard. Maybe

Daniel was right. Maybe it was as simple as following the path of his heart…

And seeing what lay at the end of that road.

CHAPTER ELEVEN

LATER that afternoon, Nick stood in his office but didn't get a lick of work done. He was working the phones but didn't pursue a single client. The pink message slips piled up on his desk, his persnickety assistant's face looking more and more concerned every time she slipped into his office and added another one to the stack. But he waved them off.

There wasn't a thing in that pile that couldn't wait until tomorrow. He had something far more important to handle.

In front of him he had the treasure map, filled with its dashed lines, all leading to one big *X*. Beneath that he had his own treasure map of sorts, though whether he'd end up finding a prize at the end or getting seriously burned still remained in doubt.

"Come on, Jerry, give me something better than that. You know you have a gold nugget sitting right in front of you that will work." Nick paused, listening to the other man. "That sounds perfect. Okay, what do you need from me on my end?" Another pause. "Consider it done."

Nick hung up the phone, then headed down the hall to the senior partner's office. Within a half hour he had called a meeting of the top partners of the law firm. He pleaded his case, laid out all the facts and, to his surprise, swayed every last one of them into supporting his project.

"I have to tell you, Nick," said Graham Norbett, one of the oldest senior partners, as he exited the room and clapped Nick on the shoulder, "that was one of the best arguments I've ever heard you make. You had such passion. Such…belief in what you were saying."

"Thank you, sir."

"It's nice to see you becoming so excited about something. So committed. Not that you aren't committed to your job, of course, but—" the gray-haired man tipped his head "—a man your age needs a passion in life, and I think you've found yours." One more clap on the shoulder, then Graham walked away.

"Mr. Gilbert," his gray-haired assistant, Harriet, said, leaning inside the room. "I hate to bother you, but you've got someone waiting in your office."

"On my way."

"All right." Harriet, who hated to get behind at work, had stress written all over her face. Nick chuckled to himself. His assistant always had her hands full keeping him on track. Whenever he went off the beaten path of how things should work, Harriet's blood pressure rose twenty points. He made a note to give her another vacation day. The woman was going to need it after this week.

As Nick started working the phones again, this time using his cell, he wondered about Graham's remarks. Finding his passion. Maybe he had. Or maybe it was just a one-day enthusiasm for something new. No way to know…at least until he proved he could pull this off. Nick kept on talking, making use of every second on the walk back down the hall to his office. "Yeah, Marty, that sounds good. I can—"

He stopped, midconversation, when he saw who sat in the dark-brown leather chair opposite his desk. "Marty? I'm going to have to call you back… Sure, two o'clock works great for me. Thanks."

He slid the phone into his pocket, entered his office and shut the door. "Carolyn. What are you doing here? Is Bobby all right?"

"Bobby is fine. I wanted to talk to you about us." She smoothed her hands over her skirt, then glanced up at him. "I realize I ran out of your house this morning without much of an explanation."

Already, he could tell by her stiff language and demeanor that this wasn't going to go well. "You did."

"I know I said I had to get to work, but really…" she smoothed her skirt again, then laced her fingers together and met his gaze head-on "—I was avoiding being alone with you. These last few days have…resurrected old feelings, and I came by to make sure that you knew there is nothing between us."

He took a seat on the edge of his desk. "Nothing. At all? Between us?"

"There's some attraction, sure, but—"

"Why are you doing this?"

"Doing what? I'm being honest."

"You're breaking up with me again. For no good reason. Again."

"I had good reasons the first time. And now."

He crossed his arms over his chest. "Okay. What are they?"

"I already told you. We can't have a relationship based solely on attraction."

"I agree. And you, Carolyn, are just talking, but nothing is coming out. What do you really want to say?"

Carolyn popped out of the seat and crossed to the window, as if she couldn't look at him anymore. She stared out at the same city that ran below her view a few blocks away. "I can't be with you, Nick. It doesn't matter if I want you or not, if we had a few days that were fun. Us being together is just not a good idea."

"And you had to come all the way over here, in person, to tell me that?"

She nodded.

He came up behind her, pausing a moment to inhale the floral notes of her perfume, then he reached out and took her into his arms, holding her to his chest. She resisted at first, then leaned into him. "Perjury," he whispered.

"No, Nick." She turned and twisted out of his arms. "It's self-preservation. It's what I do best."

"Self-preservation? Or fear?"

"Maybe both. Either way I don't get hurt. And I keep on putting the bad guys in jail. Win-win, right?"

"I only see you losing." He wanted to shake her, to force her to see what she was giving up. Frustration rose in his chest, tightening his heart. "In these last few days, I saw a side of you, Carolyn, a fun side, a laughing, happy side. You deserve that happiness. And you can balance that with your career. You know you can."

But she was already shaking her head. "I'm already happy."

"Working a million hours a week? Living

alone? Come on, don't give me that. I'm living that lie and I'm not happy."

As the words left him, he realized how true they were. He wasn't happy. He hadn't been happy in a long time.

Three years, to be exact.

He had everything a bachelor could want. The problem? The bachelor didn't want that life. He wanted the woman he'd married.

She let out a gust. "You're asking me to do the impossible, Nick. I can't."

"What's so impossible? We try again?" He closed the gap between them, cupped her jaw. "Was it that bad, Carolyn?"

Tears shimmered in her gaze, then she shook her head and they were gone. "No. But that's what made the end so much worse. I'm not going to open my heart to you and be vulnerable and have you let me down. I *needed* you, Nick, and I never need anyone. Do you have any idea how much it cost me to ask you for help that day?"

He opened his mouth, then shook his head. "I never lived your life, Carolyn. I'm not going to pretend to say I know. But if you'll let me in—"

"No. I did that and you let me down."

"I—" He cut off his sentence, then breathed out a sigh. "I did. I was young and stupid and didn't realize what being a good husband was all about. I'm sorry, Carolyn. I'm really, really sorry."

She stared at him, her lips parted in surprise. "It's all right. It's in the past."

"No, it's not all right. You needed me to understand why you had to go to Boston. I should have done that, and moreover, I should have gone *with* you. Stood by you. But I was too damned selfish, too damned focused on myself to see what you needed." He took her hands in his. "When Ronald Jakes got out of jail, and you saw his face on the screen, I don't think I realized what that did to you. I grew up with everything, Carolyn, and that made me blind. Cavalier. Insensitive. I don't think I realized fully what you went through until this week. I should have. I'm sorry."

"I…" A smile flitted across her face. "Thank you."

He cupped her jaw, his fingers trailing along her face. "You've had a hell of a life, and I admire you for what you've done with it. How you've turned a tragedy into a passion. I just don't want to see you do that at the expense of everything else."

She broke away from him, crossed her arms over her body and headed for another window. Everything about her again spelled distance. Nick couldn't understand why. "There's something else that's been bothering me ever since I saw you again. Something that's bothered me ever since I walked that out of that diner, and you…you let me go. Never fought for the marriage. For me."

"What?"

"I've prosecuted a lot of cases, Nick." She turned, put her back to the window. "I know when a defendant is holding something back. When there's that little tidbit he's left out. What aren't you telling me? Why did you give up on us so easily?"

He swallowed, and knew he had to be honest, to tell her everything. If there was ever going to be any hope of getting Carolyn back, they would have to start their relationship with good, strong honest bricks this time. "I followed you."

He watched the pieces fall into place, the numbers adding in her emerald gaze. "To Boston. When I went after Ronald Jakes again."

A faint smile crossed his face. "You asked me once if I was trying to play Lancelot when you wanted to go to Boston. I guess that's what I was doing. When I told you not to go, it was because I wanted to protect you. But you went anyway. I thought if I followed you, I could still protect you. I wanted to stop you from doing anything rash." He'd known that she'd gone out there, charged with the fire of vengeance and worry for the people Jakes had gone after, and Nick had hoped to head off Carolyn's rush to justice. "But—"

"But when you got there, I was already in the middle of the situation."

"Why did you do that, Carolyn? Risk your life with that maniac?"

She backed up, turned away and went back to the window, her breath escaping her in a long whoosh. "I thought I could help. I thought I could tell the police something about how the man thought. I thought I could stop him, bring about some miracle Hollywood ending."

"And you didn't."

"I never thought he'd do that. I never thought—" Carolyn cut off the sentence, then drew in some strength, and finished it "—he'd kill himself."

"And leave you without the closure you went there looking to get."

"I didn't go there for closure. I went there to help."

He shook his head, wishing he could get her to stop lying to herself, too. "You went there to fill those empty spots inside you. I saw it in your eyes. Saw it when you ran past the police barrier and insisted they let you help. I thought I was doing you a favor by letting you go, letting you pursue your passion, because I knew what it meant to you. I kept thinking you would find the missing pieces left by what you went through with your father. I thought if I let you go, you'd come back eventually, but all that did was allow you to bury yourself further in a hole you've never climbed out of."

"I'm not in a hole, Nick." But she looked away as she said the words.

"Oh, yes, you are. I know because I'm in the same one. For a different reason. My life is empty, Carolyn. Literally and figuratively. I live in a big empty house, a house that I now see means nothing without you in it. After you left today, I realized I didn't want to go back to what I had before. I want more."

He stayed close to her, not touching her, but close enough to inhale those floral notes, to see the tendrils of blond hair that danced around her jawline, the tears that pooled in her green eyes. "All these years, I've been searching for what I lost that day in the diner, just like you. But after this weekend, something changed for me, and now I'm prepared to make the leap and go after it. While you're still too afraid to make any changes."

She shook her head so hard, little wisps of hair escaped her bun. "I'm not afraid."

"You're more afraid than anyone I know, honey."

Her chin came up, determination setting her jaw. "Don't you understand? Every time I let someone get close, they get hurt. Like my father. I can't risk that." She shook her head, backing up, away from him. "No, Nick, it's safer this way. Safer if I just keep living my life the way I always have."

"Safer for who? For you? Because I sure as hell don't mind taking the risk." He saw her throwing up the walls again, building them so fast she was blocking any chance of them ever being together again. "Don't do this a second time, Carolyn."

"Nick, I have my career to think about. I'll be buried under cases, motions to file, briefs to prepare—"

"There will always be cases, Carolyn."

"Maybe someday down the road, we can…" She shrugged, her face crumpling a little.

And then he knew, all the pieces of this weekend, of the past three years piling on top of one another rushing at him—this wasn't just about them, it wasn't about her leaving for Boston that day. It was some bottomless debt she had never let herself finish paying.

"Oh, God, Carolyn, don't you think you've atoned enough for that day?" he said, his voice gentle, low.

She tried to hold his gaze, tried to keep her chin up, but then her lips began to quiver, her eyes filled and she had to look away. She shook her head, her fists balling at her side, Carolyn the Bulldog working so damned hard to maintain her composure, her walls. And every one of them began to fall a little at a time. "That's not what I'm doing."

Nick went to her, taking her arms, his hands sliding down to those determined fists, peeling back those fingers, slipping his hands into hers. "Oh, sweetheart, you can't stop them all."

"I'm not…" And then she was crying, really crying, and she stumbled into his arms, her tears soaking his shirt, drowning the silk of his tie. "I have to try, Nick, I have to try."

Nick just held her tight, letting the grief pour out. The realizations that the Ronald Jakeses of the world would just keep coming, day after day after day, in convenience stores and playgrounds and houses, and all Carolyn could do was try to put a finger in the dike and hope to stem the rising tide. "Carolyn, you can't stop them all," he murmured into her hair.

She shook her head, trembling in his arms. "What if I miss one? What if another child gets hurt? What if—"

Nick drew back, meeting her watery green eyes with his own. "What if you stop for one minute and live your own life? Will *that* be such a crime?"

"Look what happened to Bobby's father. That guy should have been in jail, not out on the streets with a gun. If he had been, Bobby's father would be alive today."

He stepped back, frustrated. "That's not even rational and you know it. Things like that happen everywhere. Every day. You can't stop the whole world."

"No, but I can control my corner of it." She swiped away the tears on her face. "And that's why I came here today." She swallowed, straightened her spine, resolve becoming her starch. "To say goodbye. Once and for all. I can concentrate on my job, like I always have." She drew up, shaking off the emotion, slipping into her old self as easily as a coat. "It's what I have to do."

"What?"

He hadn't seen this blow coming. Hadn't expected it at all. He'd thought he'd call her on the carpet, tell her they needed to make a choice, finally go forward or decide to grow apart, and she'd see the light and dive fully into a relationship with him. After all, they were older now, and surely, after all that had happened in the past few days, she'd seen that they could have a future. "Goodbye? But—"

"I'm sorry, Nick. I really am. But it's the smartest thing to do." She gave him a half smile. "After all, someone's gotta slay the dragons, right?"

Then she turned and left.

Telling Nick exactly what he hadn't what to hear. That he'd been dead wrong about Carolyn a second time.

But that didn't make losing her twice go down any easier.

CHAPTER TWELVE

EMPTY.

Carolyn went to work, buried herself in her job, came in early, stayed late every day, put in so many hours that three days passed without her seeing the sun rise or set.

And still it wasn't enough. Not nearly enough.

To wipe Nick Gilbert from her system.

She asked her boss for more and more cases, until he started refusing her. "I'm ordering you to take a vacation," he said.

"I can't, Ken. I need to work."

"No, you need to take time off. I know what you're doing." His light-gray eyes filled with concern. "I've seen it in myself. You're trying to burn out."

"I'm not—"

He put up a hand. "Don't argue with me. You're hoping that if you put in enough hours, you'll stop hurting over whatever it is that's got you in pain. I did it myself when my marriage started falling apart. And you know what happened? Things got worse. My wife left me, my kids stopped talking to me. Now I live with a dog that sees me only as his primary supply of food." He ran a hand through his hair, prematurely gray at forty-five. "Don't make my mistakes, Carolyn. Take some time off and fix your life. So you have one when you're my age."

She opened her mouth to argue, then saw the regrets and loneliness in his eyes. For the first time since she came to work at the city prosecutor's office, Carolyn took a look around Ken's space and noted the pictures. His ex-wife and two sons, happy and smiling on ski trips. On vacation in sunny locales. All this time, Carolyn had thought that these were family photos from Ken's life, but now she realized Ken wasn't in a single one of the pictures.

The truth slammed into her like a medicine ball to her gut. She was staring at her own empty, solitary future.

The other day she'd walked out of Nick's office, said goodbye, and chosen exactly what she was looking at right now. These pictures—it wasn't what she wanted.

But how to balance a life with the work that she

loved? The work that meant so much? The work that had defined her very self?

And in doing so, take the biggest risk of all?

Nick had taken some big risks before, but now he stood on the steps of the courthouse, about to argue the most important case of his life and convince the most difficult juror ever.

A juror who had already made her decision and might not even be open to an appeal. But he wasn't the type of lawyer who liked to lose, especially when it came to his own life.

Carolyn came through the double doors of the courthouse, a briefcase in one hand, a stack of files in the other. Mary flanked her on the right, chatting about where they should go to get a late lunch. Nick stepped in front of Carolyn and blocked her. "Miss Duff?"

Damn. Just seeing her had him ready to ditch his whole plan, take her in his arms and kiss her right here. He was sorely tempted to loosen her hair from the tight bun and run his fingers through those golden tendrils, to see the light in her eyes change from a bright green to the dark emerald of desire.

Carolyn drew up short and stopped. "Nick? What are you doing here? I thought—"

He grinned. "I'd like to present some testimony to you."

"Actually, I'm leaving court for the day. I'm going on vacation."

He blinked. "Vacation? You?"

"Boss-ordered." A faint smile crossed her lips. "But I thought it was a good idea, too."

"Do you have time for one more case?"

She took a step down, coming closer to him, sending his thoughts once again on a wild ride. "What kind of case?"

"I'd like to plead the case of you…and me."

Her face fell, frustration rising in her features. "I thought we settled that one."

A small crowd of lawyers had stopped what they were doing and were watching, making no secret of their eavesdropping. "Not to my satisfaction."

Carolyn's eyes widened, and for a second Nick thought she would protest, bolt, do whatever it took to upset his careful plan. But then the smile on her face expanded, just a little, and he knew he had a chance. "What evidence do you have, Counselor? Because I'm willing to consider an appeal, if it has merit."

"First, this." He stepped forward and stopped waiting to do what he really wanted to do. He took her in his arms, lowered his mouth to those sweet crimson lips and kissed her. She tasted of peppermint and coffee and of everything Nick dared to hope he could have again in his life.

The spontaneous gesture took her by surprise, and at first she didn't respond, which made Nick wonder if he'd done the wrong thing. Then, just when he worried he should step away, should give up on this insane idea, Carolyn melted in his arms and kissed him back.

He kept their kiss short, relatively chaste, considering they were in front of the courthouse and surrounded by most of the Lawford legal community. "May I enter that into evidence?"

Carolyn grinned. A faint redness filled her cheeks. "I'm, ah, not sure how to classify that."

He chuckled. "We can debate it later."

"Sounds like a good idea."

"My second argument," Nick said, trailing a finger down her chin, wishing he could kiss her again, "requires a field trip."

She arched a brow. "A field trip?"

He stepped back, put out a hand. "Do you trust me, Carolyn?"

A long second passed, and Nick wondered if he had lost her again. They still had a lot of unanswered questions between them. But he hoped that if he could show her this one thing, she'd understand everything about him, about what made him tick and about what was most important in life. And through that, maybe she'd find the answers to her own questions, too.

"Here, let me take these," Mary said, stepping between them and unloading all the files from Carolyn's hands and then slipping the briefcase out of her grasp. "That'll make it easier. For you to *go*, Carolyn."

"Well?" Nick asked.

"Okay. But…"

"No, buts, Carolyn. Trust me."

She hesitated a moment longer, then put her palm into his. The feel of her hand in his was like heaven, but Nick didn't count on it. Not yet. Nothing, he knew, was set in stone.

Together they walked down the courtroom steps and over to his SUV, parked in front of the courthouse. Illegally, but Nick figured one ticket was worth what he was doing today.

"Are you going to tell me anything about where we're going?" she asked.

"Not exactly." He fished in his suit pocket. "But there is a map." He handed her a piece of paper.

"What's this?"

"A treasure map, of sorts. Only it leads to someone else's treasure."

She gave him a quizzical look, then scanned the document, terribly drawn, considering he had all the art skills of a duck. "This doesn't tell me anything. There is a rule about evidentiary disclosure, you know." She buckled her seat belt and gave him a curious glance.

"You can appeal later."

She laughed. "You're breaking the rules."

"That's my specialty," Nick said, then put the vehicle in gear.

They wound through the streets of Lawford, soon leaving the downtown area behind. Nick's gut remained tight, tension holding its knot. He had no idea if everything he had worked on would pan out all right or not. Or how Carolyn would react. He'd worked solely on instinct with this particular feat of magic, pulling it all off in a matter of days.

But if he knew Carolyn the way he thought he knew Carolyn—

Then this would be what she'd been searching for. What they all had been searching for. The closure she needed, the way home.

Finally they turned down a tree-lined street and stopped in front of a small Cape-style house with a detached garage. A lush green lawn marched up a small sloping hill. A trio of pink azaleas flanked one side of the front door, a row of hedges the other. It was a simple house, as far as houses went, but perfect in so many other ways. Only one other car sat in the driveway.

"Where are we?" Carolyn asked.

"At X." Nick pointed at the treasure map, at the large capital letter that sat in the center of the paper, gave her a grin, then got out of the SUV. He came around the other side and opened the door for Carolyn. As he did, the occupants of the second car also got out. Jean Klein, Pauline Lester and Bobby.

"But…what is this?" Carolyn looked up at Nick, confusion knitting her brows.

The knot in his stomach doubled. Here went nothing. Either this impulsive plan went off without a hitch—or it all blew up in his face. During that weekend, he thought he'd gained insight into Carolyn. Insight he hadn't really had in college because he hadn't truly been paying attention. Back then, it had cost him—cost him dearly because he'd lost her.

This time he hoped he'd gotten it right, that what he had read in her, in the pockets of time when she'd opened up and let him see inside her heart, had allowed him to read what she truly needed. He took Carolyn's hand, then led her up the small walkway to meet the other trio by the front door. "We have a ceremony of sorts to attend."

"Whoa." Carolyn stopped walking and jerked Nick to a halt. "You aren't springing another elopement on me, are you?"

He studied her face, his breath caught in his chest. "Would you say yes?"

"Nick, that's not even funny. What's going on?"

"Trust me, Carolyn."

Her gaze swept over his features. Then she looked to the house, to the other people waiting for them. "All right. But if I see a minister—"

"Would it really be so bad to marry me again?" he asked, leaning forward, whispering in her ear. Thinking of the first time he had proposed—badly, he thought—on one knee in the student union of the law school. Just thinking of that clumsy, hasty proposal had him cringing. The next time he asked Carolyn to be his wife, he'd make sure he did a much better job.

She turned to face him, so close they could have kissed. His heartbeat accelerated and everything within Nick surged with desire. Damn. What was it about this woman? She drove him crazy, absolutely insane. Yet he wanted her. More with every passing second, more than he had three years ago, more than he'd ever thought possible. He must be one hell of a glutton for punishment, because she'd just broken up with him for good four days ago.

"Let's go see what's behind door number one," Nick said, then started walking again before he gave in to the urge to take her in his arms and kiss her. There were, after all, people waiting.

"Hi, Nick! Carolyn!" Bobby said when they reached him and his mother. Jean smiled at the two of them. "My momma is all better now. The doctor says she's going to be okay."

Nick and Carolyn looked to Pauline, who gave them a nod, her eyes filled with tears. Happy tears. Even Jean's eyes were misty.

Relief surged through Carolyn. A happy ending. The one she had prayed for, the one she hadn't even quite dared to hope would really come true for these two. "I'm thrilled for you," she said to Pauline, then bent down to Bobby's level. "And for you."

"And she said this year, she can be my room mom in my classroom. That means she can come have lunch with me every Thursday. That's pizza day. I love pizza."

Carolyn laughed. Such a simple thing, an ordinary, everyday kind of thing, and now, this little boy would be able to have that gift. "That's great, Bobby."

He paused, then looked up at his mother. She smiled at him and nodded. "Go ahead, ask her."

He turned back to Carolyn. "Carolyn, umm… would you come to my class someday? My teacher lets us have special people come and talk and well…" Bobby hesitated, toeing at the concrete for a moment, then his big brown eyes met hers. "Well, since your daddy died, too, I wondered if you could come when I talk about my daddy. Be my special person for that day. Because you know what it's like to not have a daddy."

The air around Carolyn stilled. Her heart squeezed. Then tears welled in her eyes and she reached out to Bobby, at first only taking his hand, but then that wasn't enough, not nearly enough to tell him how much he had touched her, opened a part of her heart, her life, that she had thought was closed, and her arms went around him. Even as the tears began to fall, to finally fall, she pulled him into her chest, holding him tight, this kindred spirit who had helped heal that last scar in Carolyn. She nodded, her tears dropping onto his T-shirt, leaving fat droplets on the cotton. "I'd love to, Bobby. I'd love to."

"Thank you," he said, but his voice was a little muffled by the hug.

A long moment passed, filled with some sniffles from all the adults, before Carolyn rose. Nick cleared his throat. "Well, I bet you're all wondering why we dragged you out here today."

"Jean said it was something to do with the Buddy program," Pauline said.

"In a way. Much more than being a buddy, though." Nick reached into his suit jacket and pulled out a large manila envelope that had been folded in half. He opened it up, then handed the package to Pauline. "This, I believe, is yours."

She looked down at the envelope, then back at him, confused. "Mine? But…what…what is it?"

"A deed."

The two words hung in the air, light as butterflies. Then they gradually filtered into her consciousness. Her eyes widened, her jaw dropped, her body froze, as if she were afraid she'd move and the whole thing would disappear. "A deed? To…" She pivoted, one inch at a time and looked at the little white house with the dark-green shutters and the wide bay window. And she started to cry. "For me? And Bobby?"

Nick nodded, a grin spreading across his face. "Yes."

Her hands went to her mouth, fingers shaking, shock all over her features. "Oh, my, no, no, you can't be serious."

Carolyn stared at Nick. A house? An entire house for Pauline and Bobby? This was way bigger than a few toys, some books from the bookstore. How had he done this and in such a short period of time? This wasn't a magic trick. This was the *impossible*.

"Look in the envelope," Nick said. "And find the keys to your new front door."

Pauline's hands were shaking so badly, Jean had to help her. The two of them reached inside, then slid out a keyring, with two silver keys hanging off it. Beside Pauline, Bobby finally started to realize what was happening. "Do we own a house, Momma? A real house? Just for us?"

Carolyn didn't even realize she was crying until the tears choked her voice. "It seems you do, Bobby. This one right here." She stared at Nick, who wasn't providing any answers. He just grinned, lighting up the spark in his cobalt eyes and emphasizing the crinkles around them. She noticed something new in his face, something she hadn't noticed before.

"It's ours?" Bobby said. "Forever? We don't have to give it back?"

"Yes," Nick said. "It's all paid for."

"*Paid for?* All of it?" Pauline's mouth opened. "How? Why?"

"My law firm, and a couple others in town, wanted to do a little more than contribute to a picnic or buy a few toys. So I made some calls."

"But this is too much," Pauline said, trying to hand the envelope back to Nick, force the keys into his hand. "We can't accept this."

Bobby stood before his mother, not saying a word. Holding his breath.

"You've been dealt a difficult hand in life, Pauline," Nick said, refusing to take the envelope or the keys. "Accept this gift and make a new start. For you and your son."

She shook her head. "There are so many other

families much more deserving than I. I can't do this, knowing that they need the money, as well. I'd much rather see you take what this costs and divide it among them."

Nick smiled. "I figured you'd say that. And I already have an argument ready. You see, my law firm makes a lot of money. Too much. And they'd like a way to offset some of those taxes. What better way to do that than help other people?"

"That's incredible, Nick," Jean said, her face wide with shock. "Just so incredible that…I don't even have words for what that's going to mean for so many families in this area."

Carolyn now realized what she was seeing in Nick. The passion he had in law school. That change-the-world belief that had attracted her to him. This was the Nick she remembered. This was the Nick she had fallen in love with.

This was the man she had been looking for over the last few days, and the man, she suspected, he had lost. He'd been merely looking for a purpose.

It was what he hadn't found in corporate law. It was what he'd always wanted. And it had taken one little boy to bring it out in him.

"You did it," she said quietly. "You changed the world."

"Not the world." Nick chuckled. "More like one

square of one street. Same as you, kind of. There's still a long ways to go."

She slipped her hand into his and gave his palm a squeeze. "You've gone miles already, Nick." Then she pointed toward Pauline and Bobby, who were inserting the key into their new house, chatting excitedly about the future, about their new life. A life that would forever be based on hope and joy. And would no longer be rooted in tragedy.

"All I need now is for you to make the journey with me, Carolyn." He turned to her. "What do you say? Are you ready to take that chance?"

CHAPTER THIRTEEN

CAROLYN had never been very good at magic. She'd tried a thousand times to memorize the little tricks that Nick had tried to teach her years before, but didn't seem to have the sleight of hand that he had. Couldn't remember the steps to the card tricks or the disappearing balls. But this time she was determined.

She'd left the new house after Pauline and Bobby had taken time to exclaim over every stick of furniture, every plant in the backyard, and asked Nick to meet her at the park that night. She'd needed some time to think, a moment to come to terms with the changes in her life.

"You have me intrigued."

Carolyn turned at the sound of Nick's voice. He strode toward her, tall, handsome, a man she now realized that she could lean on, depend on, make a partner in her life. "That was part of the plan. Keeping you on your toes."

He grinned. "This is a new side of you."

"A good side, I hope."

He closed the distance between them, and Carolyn inhaled, for a second forgetting what she wanted to say. Forgetting everything but Nick.

"Every side of you is a good side," he said.

"You showed me something today, something that made me realize there's a way to have everything I want."

"I did?"

"When you gave that house to Pauline and Bobby, I realized I could put together what I've been doing in law with helping kids like Bobby. Jean had told me I was working the wrong side of the justice system. That maybe I'd serve society better by helping these kids before they end up in the courts."

"You…want to work with kids?"

Carolyn laughed. "Yeah, I know it's insane, isn't it? I can't even make a paper bag eagle, and I'll have to learn a whole new vocabulary, but…" She smiled. "I saw what a difference it could make to a kid like Bobby. You were right."

He grinned. "Did I just hear what I thought I heard? A lawyer admitting the opposing counsel was right?"

"There aren't any witnesses to my admission so it'll never hold up in court," she teased. "But, yes,

I did. You kept telling me that someone like me, someone who had been through the same experiences as Bobby, would be the perfect person to help him. To get through to him. And today I realized I had. I saw me in him, and he, in his own way, helped me, too."

"Helped you heal the wounds of your past."

She nodded. "What if there had been someone who had talked to me about what I went through? Who had taken me out of Aunt Greta's house, even for an afternoon, and given me a bit of normalcy? Or let me know that it was okay to feel guilty about the day my father was killed? Maybe I wouldn't have grown up so afraid, so worried about the Ronald Jakeses of the world. And so convinced I had to keep repaying my father for making a sacrifice any father would have made."

Nick took her in his arms, holding Carolyn to his chest, the smile that crossed his lips telling her he approved, very much approved, of this new idea. "Not that you weren't a great bulldog, but I truly think you have a message, Carolyn, and it's been stuck inside you far too long."

She tipped her chin to meet his gaze. "We could make a good team, you know. You could do the charity end, spreading keys to houses far and wide, and I could help put together counseling and buddy programs."

"That sounds like the ideal package." His smile widened, and he dipped down to brush a kiss across her lips. "But there's only one hitch. For it to work perfectly, we'd probably have to be together all the time."

She grinned. "I thought of that. After all, haven't you always said we were better together than apart? And—" a hint of a tease appeared on her face "—since we're both lawyers, we'd need a contract for something like that, wouldn't you agree?"

"A contract?" His face fell.

But her grin only got bigger. Oh, how Carolyn was going to delight in this new side of her life. She hadn't realized until these last days with Bobby and Nick how freeing fun could be. Not until she'd stopped having it and gone back to work-only mode. But now, being able to tease Nick, actually having found a way to have it all, everything about herself felt lighter, as if she was walking on a cloud.

Carolyn stepped out of Nick's arms and waved her fingers in front of his face. "Perhaps I should try to produce a contract out of thin air?"

"Produce a contract. Out of thin air. Here in the park?" He arched a dubious brow.

She waved her fingers again, making a big production out of the movement. "I want you to know I'm serious, Nick. That this time I'm not hopping on any planes. Not running out of a diner. Not hiding in my workload." Then she slid two fingers of one hand up her sleeve in a quick, nimble movement and produced the tiny black velvet box for the engagement ring he had given her all those years ago. Not a big magic trick, as far as tricks went, but hey, she would leave the great hocus-pocus to Nick. "This is the first half of the contract. I believe you have the rest. The part that fills in all the blanks?"

His eyes widened. "You saved this?"

She nodded, a glimmer of tears slightly blurring her vision. After she had given back the rings in the diner, she had held on to the box, never able to part with that little remnant of their past. "You're not the only one who still had dreams, Nick. Who didn't give up. I just put all that away, in the back of my dresser. And pretended I didn't still hope."

"Oh, Carolyn," Nick said, sweeping her into his arms again, the box crushed in her grip. "I love you. I always have."

"And I love you, too." She lifted her lips to his, and they kissed, sealing the deal the only way Nick and Carolyn ever had. This kiss was sweeter than any before, because it brought their love full circle, had the taste of forever etched in their joining.

Then Nick leaned down and picked Carolyn

up, sweeping her off her feet. He pulled her to his chest, holding her tight, his smile wide and happy.

"What are you doing?" she asked, laughing.

"This time, I'm taking you to meet my family, because once you do, they're not going to let you get away, either. First, though, we'll stop at my house and pick up that ring. You're right. I did save it. You're not the only hopeless romantic here." He grinned, carrying her all the way back to his SUV. "And I want to do this before you have time to file an appeal, Counselor. Just in case."

"I second that motion," she said, kissing his neck, his lips, every part of Nick that she could reach. Then she noticed something and put a hand on his chest. "Wait, Nick, there's something I forgot."

"What?"

"Can we stay here and watch the sun set? I don't want to miss the beginning or end of another day for as long as I live." She twined her arms around his neck. "And I want to see every single one of them with you."

"Of course." He set her down and found a good place on the grassy knoll for the two of them to see the day come to an end. Carolyn curled into the cocoon created by Nick's arms, and as the sun's last rays cast their warmth over her skin, she

opened her heart the rest of the way to the overwhelming evidence of how absolutely wonderful
true love could be.

* * * * *

*Ladies, start your engines with a sneak preview
of Harlequin's officially licensed
NASCAR® romance series.*

Life in a famous racing family comes at a price

All his life Larry Grosso has lived in the
shadow of his well-known racing family—
but it's now time for him to take what he
wants. And on top of that list is Crystal
Hayes—breathtaking, sweet…and twenty-
two years younger. But their age difference
is creating animosity within their families,
and suddenly their romance is the talk of the
entire NASCAR circuit!

*Turn the page for a sneak preview of
OVERHEATED
by Barbara Dunlop
On sale July 29 wherever books are sold.*

RUFUS, as Crystal Hayes had decided to call the black Lab, slept soundly on the soft seat even as she maneuvered the Softco truck in front of the Dean Grosso garage. Engines fired through the open bay doors, compressors clacked and impact tools whined as the teams tweaked their race cars in preparation for qualifying at the third race in Charlotte.

As always when she visited the garage area, Crystal experienced a vicarious thrill, watching the technicians' meticulous, last-minute preparations. As the daughter of a machinist, she understood the difference a fraction of a degree or a thousandth of an inch could make in the performance of a race car.

She muscled the driver's door shut behind her and waved hello to a couple of familiar crew members in their white-and-pale-blue jump suits. Then she rounded the back of the truck and rolled up the door. Inside, five boxes were marked Cargill Motors.

One of them was big and heavy, and it had slid forward a few feet, probably when she'd braked to make the narrow parking lot entrance. So she pushed up the sleeves of her canary-yellow T-shirt, then stretched forward to reach the box. A couple of catcalls came her way as her faded blue jeans tightened across her rear end. But she knew they were good-natured, and she simply ignored them.

She dragged the box toward her over the gritty metal floor.

"Let me give you a hand with that," a deep, melodious voice rumbled in her ear.

"I can manage," she responded crisply, not wanting to engage with any of the catcallers.

Here in the garage, the last thing she needed was one of the guys treating her as if she was something other than, well, one of the guys.

She'd learned long ago there was something about her that made men toss out pickup lines like parade candy. And she'd been around race crews long enough to know she needed to behave like a buddy, not a potential date.

She piled the smaller boxes on top of the large one.

"It looks heavy," said the voice.

"I'm tough," she assured him as she scooped the pile into her arms.

He didn't move away, so she turned her head to subject him to a *back off* stare. But she found herself staring into a compelling pair of green... no, brown...no, hazel eyes. She did a double take as they seemed to twinkle, multicolored, under the garage lights.

The man insistently held out his hands for the boxes. There was a dignity in his tone and little crinkles around his eyes that hinted at wisdom. There wasn't a single sign of flirtation in his expression, but Crystal was still cautious.

"You know I'm being paid to move this, right?" she asked him.

"That doesn't mean I can't be a gentleman."

Somebody whistled from a workbench. "Go, Professor Larry."

The man named Larry tossed a "Back off" over his shoulder. Then he turned to Crystal. "Sorry about that."

"Are you for real?" she asked, growing uncomfortable with the attention they were drawing. The last thing she needed was some latter-day Sir Galahad defending her honor at the track.

He quirked a dark eyebrow in a question.

"I mean," she elaborated, "you don't need to

worry. I've been fending off the wolves since I was seventeen."

"Doesn't make it right," he countered, attempting to lift the boxes from her hands.

She jerked back. "You're not making it any easier."

He frowned.

"You carry this box, and they start thinking of me as a girl."

Professor Larry dipped his gaze to take in the curves of her figure. "Hate to tell you this," he said, a little twinkle coming into those multifaceted eyes.

Something about his look made her shiver inside. It was a ridiculous reaction. Guys had given her the once-over a million times. She'd learned long ago to ignore it.

"Odds are," Larry continued, a teasing drawl in his tone, "they already have."

She turned pointedly away, boxes in hand as she marched across the floor. She could feel him watching her from behind.

* * * * *

*Crystal Hayes could do without her looks,
men obsessed with her looks, and guys who
think they're God's gift to the ladies.
Would Larry be the one guy who could blow all
of Crystal's preconceptions away?
Look for OVERHEATED
by Barbara Dunlop.
On sale July 29, 2008.*

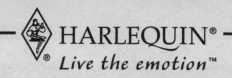

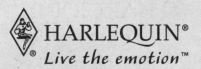

HARLEQUIN®
INTRIGUE®

BREATHTAKING ROMANTIC SUSPENSE

Shared dangers and passions lead to electrifying
romance and heart-stopping suspense!

Every month, you'll meet six new heroes
who are guaranteed to make your spine tingle
and your pulse pound. With them you'll enter
into the exciting world of Harlequin Intrigue—
where your life is on the line
and so is your heart!

THAT'S INTRIGUE—
ROMANTIC SUSPENSE
AT ITS BEST!

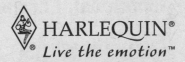

HARLEQUIN®
Live the emotion™

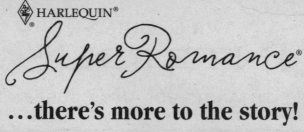

...there's more to the story!

Superromance.
A *big* satisfying read about unforgettable
characters. Each month we offer *six* very different
stories that range from family drama to adventure
and mystery, from highly emotional stories to
romantic comedies—and much more! Stories
about people you'll believe in and care about.
Stories too compelling to put down....

Our authors are among today's *best* romance
writers. You'll find familiar names and talented
newcomers. Many of them are award winners—
and you'll see why!

If you want the biggest and best
in romance fiction, you'll get it
from Superromance!

Exciting, Emotional, Unexpected...

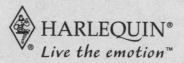